The Dubious Exploits

of a

Digital Traveller

Copyright © Geoff Baldwin 2017

ISBN: 9781973565734

Reference 151217S004

The right of Geoff Baldwin to be identified as the author of this work has been asserted by him in accordance with the Copyright, Designs and Patents Act 1988.

AUTHOR'S NOTE

Way back in the '60's and '70's hitch-hiking was a generally acknowledged way of getting about. Whether as a student heading home, a member of the armed forces going back to base or, indeed, a car delivery driver, normally showing a set of red 'trade-plates', trying to get back to a dealership.

Sadly, in the twenty-first century, with heightened levels of suspicion for anything unusual, the idea of stopping at the side of the road to allow a perfect stranger into your car would be almost unthinkable. Of course, it also works the other way, with stories appearing in the news, with frightening regularity, of people being abducted off the street and bundled into a car - some never to be seen again. It's no wonder the sight of hitch-hikers standing at the side of the road, thumbs raised expectantly is, today, almost a thing of the past.

This short tome is the story of two young lads who venture into France in the summer of '66 and the unlikely characters they meet on the way. Some of this is based on personal experiences, some is pure fiction. I will leave it to you, dear reader, to separate the wheat from the chaff!!

The story contains some explicit passages and is therefore not recommended for anyone of a prudish disposition. To everyone else, enjoy!!

All characters are purely fictional and bear no resemblance to any individuals, whether alive or dead.

PART 1

The Adventure Begins

School's (almost) Out!

I stared down at the milky white globule of fluid lying, serenely, in the soft tissue stretched across the palm of my left hand. The pulsing erection that had exploded the fluid from my loins just seconds before was now slowly, almost completely, disappearing to leave a flaccid, wrinkled, member lying, exhausted, against my thigh.

Another morning ritual completed before I rose from my bed and scrambled into my school clothes, ready to listen to my mother go through her own ritual of reminders about homework, crossing the road and "don't be lates". All while I punished the plate of scrambled eggs and mug of tea before escaping, out the door, to meet my mates on their way to school.

I made for the bathroom, my shirt tucked under my arm, ready so I could quickly wash my face over, clean my teeth and get downstairs in, hopefully, record time. Mum had already called me once and I knew that today I had to be on top form – it was the first day of our O-level finals – two years of blood sweat and tears – I didn't want to mess up. My plan was to carry on in the sixth form for the next two years, the alternative was unthinkable, an apprenticeship in a grim engineering works somewhere. I considered myself better than that, I wanted something more academic, the problem was, I wasn't that bright!

I ran a bowl of lukewarm water and quickly wiped the flannel over my face, I searched for any sign of whisker but was to be disappointed yet again. Never mind, at least there was one good thing, my days of the daily whitehead or two staring out at me from the mirror were rapidly coming to an end.

I had been lucky, spots had pestered me but not to the same extent as others in my year – I thought of poor John Elwell, six feet two inches, skinny as a rake and a face not dissimilar to the moon's surface – ravaged by craterous lumps and boils - made more-so by his unfortunate nickname, 'Disease'. But, he bore the indignity with good grace and was saved somewhat by his incredible personality and humour – he was one of the most popular pupils in our year.

I finished cleaning my teeth, making sure that I left no 'spat out' toothpaste on mum's sparkling enamel sink and had a quick pee, remembering also to pull the chain as I did so. At that moment, I remembered the crumpled piece of tissue that I had stuffed into my trouser pocket; I quickly retrieved it and threw it and its' struggling contents into the toilet bowl - to be sucked away into the whirlpool of oblivion.

"Martin!" – that's me, Martin Grady aged sixteen and seven months, five feet ten and a half inches tall with an urge to do something different with my life but, as yet undecided what it may be or how I would achieve it … anyway back to earth – "I do wish you wouldn't wipe your nose on the bed sheets, if you need to blow your nose then, for goodness sake try to remember to take a hanky to bed with you. You know where they are, in the top drawer of your dresser, I washed and ironed several of them yesterday."

I think she probably knew what the cause of the marks were but, was too prudish to mention it in front of dad. Moreover, I certainly didn't want him to find out what I was up to – somehow it didn't seem to be the thing that real men indulged in.

I gulped down the last of my tea and wiped the back of my hand across my mouth, "great thanks mum." I headed into the hall to retrieve the school bag and my coat –

although it was mid-May there was a slight chill in the air and I knew mum wouldn't let me out of the house without it. Anyhow it would be nicely stuffed in my bag before I reached the first corner of the street – best to keep the old girl happy I thought.

"Good luck for today Martin," said mum, pecking me quickly on the cheek, "what is it today, English?"

"English Lit," I mumbled back. I wasn't looking forward to this one little bit – my first O-Level paper, on a Friday of all days and my worse subject ever. How could anyone, I thought, get any pleasure out of reading George Elliot's Mill on the Floss, it was the most boring book ever. And as for Twelfth Night well, "If music be the food of love" etc then give me The Stones and Satisfaction any day.

"Well just do your best, that's all I ask," she replied and gave my shoulder an encouraging squeeze, "we'll want to hear all about it later won't we George."

There was a muted grunt from behind the Daily Express, "Good luck boy."

Frank and my other best mate, Danny Mickelburgh were already waiting when I arrived at the corner of my street and Hawthorn Crescent.

"Welcome to hell," said Danny, "did you do any more revision?"

"Nah couldn't be bothered," I lied, "waste of time even going into the examination. A fail is a foregone conclusion." In truth, I had swotted and worried, worried and swotted for nearly three hours and yet still I kept forgetting the name of Gavin Maxwell's bloody otter. As it turned out things didn't go too bad. All the names I thought I had forgotten came back to me just at the right point, during the three-hour exam, and my confidence was reasonably high when we met afterwards in the sixth form common room. We had been given permission to use the common room for the duration of the time we were taking our O's as both the upper and lower sixth were on study leave for their A's final and mock exams.

"So how did you find it?" said Frank. He was looking fairly glum but then that came as no surprise given that he had achieved perhaps the worst failure ever seen in the schools' mock English Lit examinations – even managing to spell his name wrong.

"So-so I guess. Anyhow let's get out of here I promised my mum I'd go with her to the shops this afternoon she wants to get me a couple of shirts and a rucksack for our big adventure."

"You two still planning on going through with this bloody holiday?" burbled Frank. He had never seen the point of what Danny and I were planning to do once our exams were out of the way. Or at least that's what he had said. More likely that his mum and dad had said no, he was too young to be going away on holiday on his own or even, for that matter, with his two best mates and that was the end of it!

Danny and I had been planning a holiday away for more than 6 months, in fact ever since I had received a package from the Syndicat d'Initiative de Carcassonne. I had written to the tourist office and had been sent a pile of brochures and photos of the town and had been bowled over by the beauty and splendour of the old medieval city. From that point on I had determined to go there, it was just a matter of when and, more importantly, how.

I had shared my dream with Frank and Danny and they both, if somewhat naively, said that they would love to go there one day. I had spoken with mum and dad and, while they expressed a few concerns, agreed that if I worked hard over the next few months then, perhaps they would agree to me going on holiday somewhere on my own.

We traipsed back from school saying our goodbyes at the corner. Danny had an exam in the afternoon so hadn't joined us, but he and I were meeting up on Saturday as we had some more detailed planning to discuss. We had decided to go for broke and were heading off to France for at least three weeks. This was unheard-of amongst our friends in Year-5 and we became, to some at least, ground breaking heroes or intrepid explorers. But to others we were just a couple of bragging idiots who were full of bullshit, bragging about something we would probably never end up doing. I think that, more than anything, made us both more determined to do it.

We had discussed our plans with Miss Thompson our, mouse-like, French teacher who applauded our idea but also expressed some concern that we were "a little too young" to be embarking on such a journey. In fact, when she asked for more details about where we were going to be heading for and was told Cherbourg she became quite sceptical. "So, is that it then boys, Cherbourg, where the ferry docks?"

"Well yes."

"And then what, where are you going after that, Paris, Marseille, the Cote d'Azur?" the hint of a smirk coursed across her be-spectacled face.

"Well, we're not too sure at the moment. We'll have to see what lifts come along."

"Lifts? What do you mean lifts, is this how you plan on getting about over there? Are you planning on hitch-hiking? Have you discussed this with your parents?"

"Um, yes, well we have mentioned it to them and they have said to be careful. Anyhow we won't have enough money for trains or buses or anything like that."

"Well, if your parents are happy about then I guess there is nothing I can say other than to echo their words and say be careful," she stood up, signalling the end of our conversation, "and don't forget to send me a card."

****

Saturday morning woke with glorious sunshine pouring through my bedroom window. I leapt out of bed, my morning routine forgotten. Today we had plans to fulfil, and I had told Danny that I wanted to be ready to get out on the road as soon after nine as possible – today we were planning to hitch down to Southampton docks to buy our ferry tickets to Cherbourg!

I had been saving hard for ages, squirreling away every-last penny from my paper round which mum had insisted I give up some six months ago, to concentrate on my studies. I had objected saying that I would do extra revision in the evening. But she wouldn't relent, and, in the end, I had broken the news to "Pop" McCarthy, the old boy who ran the newsagents. "It's a shame Marty." Pop had said on my last day, "we'll all miss you and I know Mrs Jobson has always had a soft spot for you." He gave me a knowing wink.

Mrs Jobson – Daily Telegraph, The Lady and, on Tuesdays, The Woman's Realm - a buxom woman, showing the first signs of middle-age, lived up at the Manor.

Delivering to her door was always a game of cat and mouse and I always felt like the poor rodent! The drive leading to her imposing front door gave me no opportunity for cover and in the two years as her delivery boy I never once managed to get away without being accosted by her – I imagined her being a lusting man-eater in her younger days but, she was a generous tipper when it came to Christmas!

I remember my first day, I had left my bike at the imposing double gates and walked the thirty yards or so to the house, drawing the paper and magazine from my sack in readiness to shove them through her letter-box. But I never managed it – the door was hastily wrenched open as I was in mid-thrust and I was greeted by a large apparition, dyed blonde bouffant hair, flouncy pink silk gown barely covering a pair of huge bosoms, bouncing happily in completely opposite directions to each-other. Under her arm a small white dog, complete with pink bow, yapped at me while at the same time being battered across the head by a pendulous right bosom as the whole woman shook with apparent glee at seeing me.

> There was a young lady from Devizes
> Whose boobs were of two different sizes
> The left one was small, hardly noticed at all
> But the right one was **huge** and won prizes

"Hellooo dear boy I haven't seen you here before now have I, are you new?" I had glumly nodded affirmation. "Would you like to pop in for a little glass of lemonade or something?" her bosom bouncing knowingly. But her mouth turned down when I stammered that I had to finish my round and get off to school. "Never mind my sweet plum perhaps another time then," and she gave me a knowing wink.

From that day on I ran the gauntlet of Mrs Jobson. I would spot the rustle of the net curtain on the upstairs landing window – and a brief second later the door would be flung open as she waited, almost gleefully, for me to drop the paper into her outstretch hand while her dog yapped at me from the other.

I had tried every way I could think of to avoid her, even at one stage, climbing over the garden wall and dashing across the manicured lawns, dodging from shrub to shrub like a junior James Bond. But each time I had failed, it was almost as though she had a sixth sense for sniffing out the enriched testosterone in a young, adolescent male.

Danny called at our house at the agreed time and we set off to position ourselves in the right spot on the main road heading towards Southampton. We only had to travel some thirty miles but when you are relying on your thumb and the generosity of others it could be a thousand. We were also limited by time as both our sets of parents had insisted that we be home by three in the afternoon "or you'll be for the high jump my lad", as my dad had put it. He and mum were having a rare evening out at a new Chinese restaurant that had just opened in Winchester – they were meeting my Uncle Jim and Auntie Kath at five, so I had better not be late as I was looking after my twelve-year-old brother Brian, oh what joy.

As luck, would have it we didn't have too long to wait for our first lift and we were taken directly into Southampton. Our benefactor was an elderly vicar and his, equally elderly wife. His car, an old Ford Anglia pulled up almost alongside us, the window wound down and he stretched across his wife to look us up and down. "Good morning gentlemen can we help you at all?" We explained our situation and he told us that, as they were going that way, they would be more than happy to give us a lift.

"Jump out Edith," he said to his elderly and somewhat large spouse, "let the boys get into the back."

Edith opened the door and smiled up at me, "you'll have to give me a bit of help please dear." She extracted her rather large, cumbersome, legs from the foot-well and reached out her hand for me to grab hold of. I gingerly pulled her up but, with combined sweaty palms, our hands parted company just as she almost reached the full vertical position and she fell back into her seat with an oomph and a cackle of laughter from her husband still sitting inside the car. At the same time, I was greeted with an eye-full of brown stocking tops, kept in place by wide elastic suspenders cutting into ample white thighs!

Our second attempt at extricating Edith was a little more successful and we both made ourselves comfortable in the back of the car smirking quietly to ourselves at the unfortunate situation our benefactors wife had found herself in.

"So, what are you boys going to be doing in Southampton?" asked the reverend. We explained the reason for the visit and told him of our plans for when we had finished our exams.

"Well in that case we shall take you direct to the ferry offices and then, if you wish, I shall drop you back off on the Midhampton road. We have plenty of time on our hands, we're only going to a small garden party at the Bishop's residence and then off to Winchester to try the new Chinese restaurant that's just opened."

"Two more for the Chinese, maybe they'll meet mum and dad," I thought, "must be the in-place for the middle-aged and elderly."

Edith giggled, "I may even try those new-fangled chopsticks."

I smiled indulgently, even as a sixteen-year-old schoolboy, I knew that the Chinese had been using chopsticks for several thousand years! Old people had so much to learn about life.

We hadn't really thought too much about what we would do after we had bought our tickets but, with my time limited by dad's rather un-subtle threat not to be late, I was more in favour of coming straight back. And anyway, they were a nice old couple and it seemed to me that they would possibly be upset if we had refused their offer. It seemed to me that tonight, every level of society was going to be represented at the Great Wall - or whatever it was called.

With ferry tickets safely stashed in our pockets and having been given a lift back to the Midhampton Road by the kindly vicar and his wife we made good time on the journey home, getting to within five miles of our destination in just over an hour. As we waited for a car to come along which would hopefully take us on the final leg Danny spotted a Number thirty-three coming along.

"Hey that will take us right past my road," he quipped, "shall we hop on?"

I felt I had to make one point clear. "Look you know we won't be able to do this when we're in France, don't you? We just won't have the money to jump on the first bus or train that comes along."

He gave me a look that suggested I was being totally unreasonable but at the same time talking adult-like sense. "Yeah ok-ok, just thought it may save us a bit of walking and it's fairly built up here. Cars can't always see us here, with so many others parked on the side of the road."

I realised that what he was saying actually made sense and agreed that maybe taking the bus was not such a bad idea. It was at this point that we both realised that the bus was looming closer and, of course, we had no idea where the bus-stop was. So, jumping up and down we tried to catch the drivers' attention as it sped past on its way to Danny's street. All our efforts were in vain, the driver took no notice of the two foolish idiots gesticulating at him from the pavement and we were treated to whoops, waves and V-signs from a group of Midhampton Grammar fourth-formers who happened to be sitting on the top of the bus – Monday morning at school was going to be so embarrassing.

****

The following three weeks at school dragged by as the exams came and went, some more successful than others. Generally, I felt that things hadn't gone too bad – they certainly could have been a lot worse! But now, at last, we were free; free of the pressure of continual revision and endless hours spent in the school gym sitting, under the stares of the exam invigilators as they paced like silent wraiths between the rows of bent heads and scratching pens.

The month of June was fast drawing to an end and Danny and I were in the final stages of planning. This took the form of what we would be carrying rather than where in France we would be going. Our mums had decided that it would be too expensive to buy food and so had bought large amounts of packet dinners including chow miens, curries and other strange looking recipes which just needed water adding. A small cooker thus became an essential part of our equipment together with several spare gas cylinders – we couldn't afford to run out of that, the very thought of having to eat a beef curry re-hydrated with cold water sounded decidedly unappetising! And so apart from a few clothes, the parental assumption being that we would be doing our own laundry so not too much was needed, our other essential was my small bivouac tent that I had used when going on holiday with mum and dad for the past five years. It was rather tatty but still serviceable and we were working on the assumption that France would be hot and dry and so the idea of it leaking never occurred to us.

Money was going to be an important issue. I had emptied my post-office savings bank of the sixty-seven pounds I had managed to save and, together with a further ten pounds' emergency fund generously donated by dad I felt quite flush, especially, when converted, the amount came to over seven hundred francs – it was easy to get carried away.

One of our friends had suggested that perhaps we should think about looking for work grape picking in the southwest of France but, unfortunately when we enquired it would have been too early in the season;

the grapes wouldn't be ready for a few weeks yet. So, what we carried with us would have to do but, we also needed to ensure we kept money aside for our return tickets.

At last, the day of our departure arrived! Our ferry was due to leave Southampton at eight in the evening and Danny's mum and dad had agreed to take us down to the docks. They arrived in plenty of time so that between them, mum and Mrs Mickelburgh could sit us down and give us our final pep talk.

"Now remember, don't get into any trouble with any French boys or girls and be polite to people you meet over there. And if you don't feel comfortable with any of the people who may stop to give you a lift then don't get in, you never know what sort of people are out there."

We knew it was useless to put up any sort of argument so sat dumbly, nodding in all the right places. We ventured a quick glance at each-other at the mention of strange people stopping to pick us up – the same thing was going through our minds, our friend Franks, his dad was a real weidro!

"Right then you two, I think it's time we were heading off." Said Danny's dad.

I could see tears starting to well up in mum's eyes, but she disguised it well by grabbing hold of me and hugging me close. I acknowledged with a hasty peck on the cheek – I didn't want Danny to think I was some sort of wimp. Mum pulled back and made to smooth her dress down.

"You boys take care now and we'll see you both very soon. Brian for heavens' sake, please – your finger!" My brother separated his index finger from his left nostril where, for the past few weeks, it had seemed to take up permanent residence – at least, on this occasion, it was not accompanied by any content.

Mr Mickelburgh laughed, "you'd better be careful young man, that you don't start pulling out your brains. Or you'll end up sounding loike an Oirishman!" Brian stared at him with a look of confusion, disbelief and pre-pubescent disdain. He neatly side-stepped Mr Mickelburgh's wavering hand as he tried to ruffle Brian's hair and then stepped back hastily, a somewhat embarrassed look spread across his face, realising he had encroached into Brian's personal space.

It was nothing compared to the look on mum's face, a Galway girl to the heart. "Come on you two," she said, giving the poor man a look that could have frozen over hell. Thankfully it prevented any possible outburst from

Brian, "time you were all getting off. You boys don't want to miss that boat do you."

Danny's mum smiled and added her support. Mr Mickelburgh gave a polite and slightly embarrassed cough and made to get into his car, hesitating, at the last minute, to shake hands with mum and dad, mouthing a quiet "sorry" and with a promise that they would keep in touch over the next few weeks while we were away.

Danny and I bundled into the back seat of the car and with my face pressed against the back window I waved my goodbyes. I felt exhilarated, but a little hesitant, I was sure all of this was a good idea but, a little nagging in the back of my mind was asking me whether I, we, were doing the right thing. I turned to Danny, who also seemed to be lost in his own thoughts, "Well here we go," I said, "in for a penny, in for a pound." He grinned back at me but couldn't disguise the worry in his eyes.

****

We sat together in the foot-passengers waiting area watching cars, on the other side of the large glass partition, slowly stream pass as they queued up waiting to be checked in by immigration control. Our plans for what we would do when we disembarked at Cherbourg were still somewhat vague and haphazard - basically there was only one direction to head and that was south.

There were several others also waiting with us including, quite a number lugging large backpacks similar to our own. This, we assumed, meant that there may be some significant competition for lifts once we left the ferry port and so we quickly decided to keep an eye open for any likely looking cars and their drivers who may be amenable to picking us up. This, of course, didn't mean that we intended to ask them directly, more to make them aware of our presence on the boat.

Danny quickly spotted a potential mark and nudged me as a red Mini Cooper stopped opposite to where we were sitting. The car was driven by a man, probably in his early twenties, clearly travelling alone and a great possibility for taking us out of the town and on our way to wherever.

Very soon the request for foot passengers to board the ferry came over the public-address system – this was it, we were about to depart English soil! We hoisted our rucksacks onto our shoulders and joined the queue of passengers as they headed across the short stretch of tarmac to where the, huge side of the ferry loomed up before us. The lights playing across the dock-side made the bulk of the boat almost terrifying as we mounted the gangplank to be swallowed up into the belly of the leviathan.

We followed the crowd of foot passengers through what seemed an endless maze of corridors until we suddenly emerged into a brightly lit area of tables and seats many already occupied. We hurried through the crowd trying to avoid barging into the crowd with the awkward rucksacks that bounced around on our backs. I spotted another couple of blokes who, similar to us, were carrying their homes on their backs. They were heading hurriedly towards an empty table. I turned and hissed to Danny, "Quick there's a place over." I raced forward, determined to beat the others, knocking over a chair containing a young kid in the process.

"Oi, watch yerself - awkward sod," came a voice from an indignant mother who was busy scooping up the screaming infant into her arms. I grinned in embarrassment and mouthed an awkward apology to the woman before resuming my desperate surge to reach the empty table.

The others had taken advantage of my temporary disablement and were almost there when I spotted Dan leap in from the other side and claimed the two seats just seconds before they got there. He laughed up at them and flicked them a quick V-sign as they turned away muttering "jammy bastard" under their breath.

We took our seats, dropping the rucksacks next to the chairs. I reached down and extracted a partially crushed packet of ten Gold Leaf from the top pocket of the rucksack and lay them triumphantly on the table.

"How many did you manage to get?" asked Dan.

"A full house." I smirked and flipped open the top of the box to reveal the ten little tubes of heaven neatly lined up waiting to be puffed on in the coming hours.

I had been quietly filching dad's cigarettes, one at a time over the past couple of weeks ready for just this occasion. I had kept my nicotine habit quiet from mum and dad but now I was away from mum's steely gaze I could relax and enjoy the many freedoms that lay ahead. I had suggested to Danny that he do the same but, as his dad rolled his own, he said it was more awkward so it was all left up to me.

My dad used to roll his own but when he received his promotion into management he decided that the time was right to move up to tailor-mades. Unfortunately, he now considered that roll-your-owners, together with those sporting tattoos, belonged to a lower social order, including Dan's dad who was still working on the shop-floor.

However, this was not borne out by his own personal habits when within the security of his own home. I dreaded it when mum had made a blackberry crumble – I would sit and wait, watching for dad's face to contort into a grimace as the seeds began to interfere with his teeth, his mouth twisting around until he could stand it no longer and pushed out his false teeth into his hand where he would make a show of licking around the plate to remove the offending irritants. The teeth would then be placed on the dining table with as much reverence as our local vicar gave to the communion offertory, all the while dad would continue sucking and swilling the remainder of his pudding into his toothless jaws. Finally he would finish with a relaxing belch before scooping up his gnashers and push them back into his mouth, taking the time to make a slight snapping action to ensure they were seated properly. We looked around us, searching out the bloke in the Mini Cooper, he was nowhere to be seen. Just then and without any warning the boat gave a barely visible judder and, before we realised what was happening, we started to move. We watched through the windows as the lights on the dockside slowly moved past us and then there was a muffled roar as the ferry manoeuvred around as it lined up with the main harbour channel and set its sights for the open water. We stared at each-other, not uttering a word, this was it, just us two and no going back. We continued to look out for the next hour, each with our own thoughts as the lights of England and home disappeared into the distance and before us lay the inky darkness of the English Channel – next stop Cherbourg. Already I was beginning to feel homesick but pride, stubbornness, call it what you will, refused to allow me to share my inner thoughts with Danny. Instead I comforted myself with the idea that he may be having the same doubts as me.

As we settled back into the uncomfortable chairs to try and get a bit of rest, it was here that we planned to spend the night – no luxury cabins for us – Mini Cooper-man walked past our table. As he did so I spotted his passport hanging by a thread out of the back of his jeans pocket. In a trice, it had fallen out without him noticing – I seized my chance, jumped out of my seat, scooped up the passport and dashed up behind him. "S'cuse me," I said, a little breathlessly, "I think you dropped this."

He turned around, saw the passport in my hand and felt in his back pocket. "Oh, thanks mate," he smiled as I handed back the errant passport – I took the opportunity.

"You're in the mini right?"

"Yeah, what of it?" he replied

"Oh," I felt a little flustered, "we just saw it drive on board, we're big fans of minis." I couldn't think of anything else to say.

"Yeah, they're alright. Anyway, thanks for picking this up mate." He put the passport back into his pocket and disappeared along a corridor, making for the cabins. Well, I had done as much as I could. Everything else was now in the lap of the gods.

****

Cherbourg to who knows where!

Six in the morning, an un-earthly hour for any young man to be rudely awaken by a metallic voice echoing through the boat that foot passengers should prepare to dis-embark in fifteen minutes. The trip over had been uncomfortable and, while I hadn't been sick, my insides felt in turmoil and I had a thumping headache. Sleep had only come much later in the night – I needed water. We stumbled to our feet and, hoisting our rucksacks onto our shoulders, joined the milling throng of bleary-eyed foot passengers slowly following the exit signs.

French immigration was non-existent, and we passed out through the dock-gates where we saw a sign showing "Toutes Routes – Sud". Our schoolboy French was sufficient to know that meant one thing – South and the sun, our earlier fears and homesickness had disappeared. It was the beginning of our French adventure!! It was going to be a great day! The sun was peering above the surrounding buildings – it was going to be a hot one too!

Ahead of us, as we trudged up the road, were the two blokes who had lost out to us on the race for the table the last evening.

"Let's stop here," I said to Danny, "best if we keep first in the queue as the cars come out."

"Oi! You two!!" a shout told us we had possibly made our first mistake, "get your arses behind us - fuckwits." An aggressive thumb suggested we carry on past them and move further up the road.

"Better do as they say," said Danny, "they look like they mean business and they're bigger than us too."

We picked up the rucksacks and hesitantly walked towards them, they stood there staring at us, they looked like students with wispy beards open-toe sandals but had the attitude of bull-necked body guards – we certainly weren't going to argue with them. They stood to one side as we passed them. I heard a muttered "fucking kids", as we carried on up the road but decided that discretion was the better part than valour so kept my mouth firmly shut.

We positioned ourselves a further fifty yards up the road and dropped the rucksacks, thankfully, onto the verge just as the first of the cars and lorries started trundling out of the dock gates. We stuck out our thumbs and smiled expectantly at the approaching traffic – no luck just a couple of waves from smiling drivers and their passengers as the passed us by, some even gave us a thumbs' up. "Thanks," I muttered, "for nothing."

Suddenly, out of the dock gates I saw the Mini Cooper accelerate up the hill coming towards us – he shot past the two blokes and continued to speed towards us and then, out of the blue and with a screech of tyres stopped ten yards beyond where we were standing. The guy turned back and beckoned to us – we couldn't believe it, last evening had worked, he'd remembered! We watched, with mouths open, as he leaned over and opened the front passenger door and beckoned to us. "Quick!" I shouted, and we almost dragged the rucksacks over to the car.

He leaned over the passenger seat, looked up to us and said, "Wanna lift guys, where you goin'?"

"Uh dunno," I stammered, "just heading south."

"Me too," came the reply, "well jump in then, haven't got all day."

He tipped the seat forward and I pushed Danny into the back seat, followed by both rucksacks. I pulled the front seat forward and, just before getting in, looked back to where the other two hitchers were stood staring at us incredulously. I savoured the moment for a few brief seconds, flicked them a cheeky V-sign and hopped in - we were on our way!

The mini came to a juddering halt. "Ok lads here you are, Fouras is about twenty kilometres that way, I'm heading in that direction. Don't forget to roll your arses when chatting up the local girls!" Dave, our host/chauffeur since leaving Cherbourg laughed loudly as he slammed the car door shut, revved the engine and was gone in just a few brief seconds and a cloud of dust.

We had been travelling for almost eight hours and were now sitting on a quiet country road somewhere near La Rochelle in west France. We had taken a bit of time to study our dog-eared map of France during our journey and decided that the small seaside town on the west coast may be a good place to be our first stop.

We had had a great time driving down through the French countryside with Dave. He had given us our first real lesson on life in France and it was on his recommendation that we head for Fouras. Forget sitting in a stuffy classroom, repeating French verbs for forty-five minutes every couple of days, this was the real macoy and we were starting to love it.

We had stopped in a small country town on the way down and Dave had taken us into a small transport café for a typical French lunch. We had found a table in the bustling café and the smiling waitress indicated a blackboard showing various choices of food for the discerning traveller.

"What's a 'crock musheur'?" demanded Danny (he was mind numbingly useless at French)

"It's called a Croque Monsieur," replied Dave, "roll your 'R' in croque, almost like you're gargling. That way you won't make an arse of yourself when you order it. Basically, it's a toasted ham and cheese sandwich, it's delicious."

I laughed. "That's it Dan, roll your arse when you order your food then you won't make a bigger arse of yourself." I sniggered at my own joke, "but you might get a few funny looks from the natives." Dave smiled but Dan just sneered.

"Piss off," he muttered – and he got his revenge several minutes later!

I felt my stomach churning again – I had tried to ignore it for as long as I could but now it had reached the point of no return. "Any idea where the bog might be?" I made it as a cool, calm comment but was beginning to feel desperate.

"Yeah, it's through the door over there," replied Dave, "mind the rats," he laughed. I scraped the chair back and rose to my feet taking care to keep the cheeks of my arse closed tightly together as I walked towards the back of the café.

I walked through a grimy looking door displaying "Toilet" and found myself in a dark lobby with two equally grimy doors one with a bonnet stencilled on the door, the other a top-hat. I pushed the top-hat open and was knocked back sideways by the stench. The room was barely big enough to swing a cat, but I couldn't take in any more, I needed to get to the stall lurking in the corner fast before I exploded.

I pushed open the door and stopped short before I fell into the black maul of a hole that greeted me. I had never seen anything like it before in my life – two raised footprints set astride the hole guided me to the stooping position I would have to assume to aim my backside in the right direction. I stepped gingerly onto the footprints and undid my jeans and prepared to pull them and my pants down. But how could I ensure that I would just mess into my pants? How would I explain it to Danny and Dave waiting for me out in the café?

I decided that I would stoop down and use my hands to push my pants as far forward as I could. But my balance was not feeling too good and I began swinging backwards and forwards as I stooped and my aim for the hole was not always on target.

The reason for me being there suddenly came to life. I had been temporarily bunged up by the sight that had greeted me but, now natural forces had taken over and I emptied my bowels around the grubby porcelain bowl with the bare minimum actually reaching its target. But I didn't care, the relief was instantaneous, and I finished off the process with a long luxurious pee. I had managed to regain my balance and just allowed myself to rest there until I had ensured that nothing more was going to happen before pulling at the thin paper roll to clean myself up.

Having finished I pulled my pants and jeans up and prepared to flush. I stepped off the footprints and reached for the chain which rested against the back wall. I had to lean right across the evidence of my upset stomach and realised I would have to step back on to the footprints. But then I realised the chain was not long enough for me to be able to step back onto terra-firma before flushing. I would have to pull the chain and then step back – it was going to have to be one smooth, fluid movement. I prepared myself to pull, fearful that the water would wash over everything including the footprints. I made sure the door was unlocked, knowing I would have to jump for it – there was no point in delaying it, I had already been in there for what seemed like ages.

I pulled down on the chain and prepared to jump out of the way as a deep gurgling roar was immediately followed by a rush of water shooting out from all four corners of the bowl. The recently evacuated contents of my body were immediately swept around into a whirlpool that whooshed toward the footprints giving me a fraction of a second to get out of the way. I stood there, transfixed as the water poured over the footprints only to be instantly sucked down into the hole to end up who knows wear.

I had survived my first encounter with a French toilet and was quite pleased with myself as I unbolted the door until, that is, I realised that no water came out of the old tap dangling over the wash basin. I was mortified, mum had always insisted that I remembered to wash my hands after using the loo and now I had to have something to eat – what could I do?? I headed back into the café and sat back down at the table.

"Feeling better," asked Dave, "was it any good in there?" he smiled.

"Certainly, a lot different to anything I've seen before." I replied.

"What d'you mean?" questioned Danny.

"You'll have to find out for yourself," I laughed, "actually I think I need a drink of water, can you order one please Dave?"

"Yeah sure," he replied, "what no wash basin?" he winked.

"Something like that," I replied, glad that he was with us. He understood the French way of life, that was obvious.

****

The road was ominously quiet, we had been standing at the junction for a full thirty minutes and not one car had passed us. I began to think that we could be stuck here for the remainder of our holiday. Panic welled up inside of me, how would we get home – homesickness was beginning to take over.

"Come on," I said to Dan, "there's no point in hanging around here, we may as well start walking."

Danny made no effort to get up from where he sat on the side of the road. "It's so bloody hot," he grumbled, "don't you think we may have come a bit too far?"

I realised immediately that he was feeling the same as me – a little unsure of what he had got himself into and missing his home and mum and dad as much as I was. I knew that one of us had to be a little more upbeat.

"Yeah, I know what you're saying Dan, but we need to

find somewhere to camp down for the night and then make plans in the morning. I don't know about you but I'm feeling a bit peckish too. Come on let's get going we can't hang about here."

Our saviour came some twenty minutes later when we caught the sound of something akin to a large lawn-mower getting closer and closer and then, a few seconds later, around the corner came an old Citroen 2CV van valiantly negotiating the barely perceptible incline we had walked up effortlessly, even though we were weighed down by the rucksacks. We quickly dropped them to the ground, stuck our thumbs out and put on our best smiles.

We were in luck, although I wasn't sure whether the car stopped for us or that it was just giving up the ghost. But my fears were unnecessary when a curly head stuck itself out of the passenger window and shouted "Ou allez vous?"

I wasted no time, ran up to the car and said "Fouras," in my best Franglais – making sure I rolled my arse! "Anglais?" came the response – I nodded. "OK get in." He flicked a thumb behind him, indicating we should climb in through the rear door of the old van, getting out as he did, so he could close the doors behind us.

Getting into the back of the van was not as easy as we expected, we were sharing the limited space with several crates of live chickens and the smell was overpowering, a mixture of bird shit and Gauloises cigarettes. But we couldn't care less; we were on the last stretch of our days' journey – our French adventure had well and truly begun.

"You are on yer vacances, yes?" asked the guy who was attempting to keep the old van going by rapid changes of gear and deft use of the accelerator.

"Yeah, we're seeing real France," I replied, trying to sound cool, "how about you, are you on holiday or working?" I assumed they were working seeing as they had a van load of chickens in the back with us. One of whom was clearly quite hungry as it was desperately trying to remove the sock from my foot – I kicked at it unceremoniously.

"Non, we werk as waitresses in an 'otel in Fouras. Monom is Julien et ziss is mon ami, Bernard." He turned around to shake our hands at the same time pulling the steering to the left. The van swerved violently across the middle of the road, fortunately for us nothing was coming in the opposite direction!

We were thrown across the back of the van as Julien valiantly tried to regain control, but it was too late. One of the cages, heavily laden with chickens lost its balance and tumbled onto the floor of the van. Suddenly the little car was full of flapping, squawking birds - feathers flying in all directions. I turned to look for Danny and came nose to beak with an indignant bird which had perched itself on my shoulder. We stared at each other for a few brief seconds before I realised what was happening. I hated chickens unless they were lying on a dinner plate covered in gravy. I tried to push the bird off, but it was going nowhere, it's claws firmly attached to my tee-shirt, a beady eye giving me a challenging stare almost like it was itching for a fight!

"OK monsieur ainglish," it squawked, "what is your next move?" It was laughing at me, feathers raised in an air of French-poultry aloofness!

"Watch it buster," I hissed, "or I'll wrap my hands round your scrawny next and stretch it from here to next week." But it was too late my protagonist got in the first blow, a vicious peck to my ear – I was lucky it wasn't my eye, I had turned my head back just in time.

"Get this bloody thing off me!" I almost screamed - I felt like a very reluctant Long-John Silver. If I had a crutch I would have brained the damn bird!

The van came to a juddering halt and Danny, me and the chicken shot forward together with two cages and half a dozen loose chickens. Danny came to rest with his head hanging over Julien's shoulder, he turned to look at the startled Frenchman, "Bonjour," he said, "I'm appled Dan, how do you do."

Julien looked at him and a huge smile covered his face, "Ello Anglais, welcome to La France."

We burst into fits of laughter, the chickens and mess in the van temporarily forgotten. The other francais, Bernard, was the first to speak, "Oh merde! Restez la!"

"Ee's saying stay there – we will make it better." Julien smiled at us as he jumped out of the car and ran around to the back.

Bernard pulled the door open and jumped in next to us, pulling the door closed behind him. He proceeded to move around the cramped space desperately trying to catch the fluttering, panic-stricken, chickens – grabbing them by any means possible and quickly shoving them back into the cages. Eventually, after a hectic few minutes, all the chickens were once again, where they belonged and Danny and I could relax once more as les francais clambered back into the front of the van. Julien turned the key in the ignition - Nuuurrrr, nuuuuuuurrrrrr narumphhh chaaaaa chhhaaaa dunnn ddunnnnn duuun and the poor little car finally chugged into life. There was a graunching noise as Julien pulled the strange looking gearstick into first and the car lurched forward - we trundled on our way.

Bernard leaned round with a packet of open cigarettes in his hand, "fumee?"

I gratefully accepted, feeling that we had earned it. I noticed that the cigarettes had no filter and carried a distinctive smell, but I thought, "when in France …" I cupped my hands around the ciggie as Bernard offered up a lighted match - I drew in deeply. Now I am not an experienced smoker, only managing to grab a hasty puff when my dad wasn't looking and, of course, nicking a few if the opportunity comes my way. As I drew the smoke down into my lungs, the strength of the cigarette made me feel dizzy, my head began to spin, I coughed – long drawn out fits of coughing that seemed to go on and on. My eyes started to feel sore and began watering, I leant back against the side of the van the feeling in my stomach warned me that sickness lay just around the corner. The van sides rattled against my pulsing head until I could take it no longer and lay down on my side waiting for the sensations to subside.

"Ce Gauloise, is good, non?" laughed Bernard

I looked at him through my watering eyes, "Oui," I muttered but he knew I didn't mean it and laughed even more. "I managed to look over at Danny, "Wanna finish it?" I spluttered.

"Yeah pass it over," he replied, "some of us can take it." I gratefully handed over the Gauloise which, by this time, had burned halfway down. Danny took a long, deep drag, I could tell by the tip which glowed bright red. He inhaled and blew out a dense cloud of sweet smelling smoke – it had no effect on him at all, the bastard!

"Hey this is good," he laughed and took another drag. It really hacked me off. How could it have no effect on him but made me feel like death? I felt that my manly influence had been assaulted and was determined to not let it get the better of me. I decided I would buy a pack at the earliest opportunity and work at it until my lungs and throat could take it.

****

Fouras

"Completez ce carte la!!" the sour-faced woman behind the reception desk at 'Le Camping Touristique' thrust two printed cards into my outstretched hand.
I smiled and muttered a quiet "merci", before handing one to Dan, "Just fill this thing in mate, you know the usual – name, address, passport details, how long we're planning to stay. My dad told me we'd have to do this, it's the rule in France."
"Bloody hell what a waste of time," grumbled Danny, "what do they expect us to do, rob a bloody bank or something?"
"Just do it!" I replied, "then we can find a pitch for the tent and I can get a bit of sleep, I feel knackered."
And I was right – we had been travelling all day and had just walked a couple of kilometres in the blistering late afternoon sunshine, I could feel the hot sun burning into the back of my neck and remembered mum's warning about getting burnt – added to that I didn't want to end up like a well-cooked lobster, that certainly wouldn't do much for my street-cred with 'les mademoiselles'.
Julien and Bernard had dropped us just outside the restaurant where they worked with apologies that they

couldn't take us any further as they were already late and expected to be 'bollocked' as it was for the mess in the back of the van. We had said our goodbyes and they had invited us into the town that evening, which happened to be their day off, with a promise of showing us around and maybe meeting some pretty girls too. We thanked them with an air of bravado, but I think we were both a bit worried that perhaps we were biting off a little more than we could chew …. but we would go and see what happened, after all – when in Rome. We finished filling out the cards and handed them back to misery-guts.

"Passports!" she glared at me holding her hand out. "It's ok, she only wonns to make sure what you 'ave written on the registration card matches what's in your passport." The sexy, slightly throaty, feminine voice behind us set my heart racing, I spun around and was greeted by an apparition of absolute beauty. Her deep blue eyes bore into me, she was stunning and perhaps only a year or so older than us. Her hair was a startling blonde and she had been kissed by the sun giving her skin a warm honey glow. She was wearing a tiny white tee-shirt stretched provocatively over small, pert breasts and fashionably hot, hot-pants out of which sprouted impossibly long legs. It was clear that she had nothing on under her shirt from which my eyes were unable to remove themselves.

I was completely smitten and immediately dreamed of the potential for cementing our union - then I spotted him - the equally stunning Adonis standing a couple of metres behind her. He stood a good few inches taller than me and possessed the type of body I could only dream of owning, this guy really worked out!

> *So fair her face, so fair her hair*
> *So fair her pulsing figure.*
> *But not so fair, the maniacal star of her*
> *boyfriend who's much bigger.*

She came up and stood directly in front of me, "Hi I'm Marie-France."
"Hi, I'm Marie-France", those four simple words left me completely transfixed. She had an impossible to imagine accent, certainly not from our neck of the woods – far more exotic! I felt myself blush and kicked myself inwardly at how stupid I must look.
"Oh, err yes of course, that's what I guessed she wanted it for, just trying out my French you see, haven't had much chance to use it, we only arrived in France this morning - heading south, not sure where yet but we plan on just chilling out for a few weeks, maybe longer see how the land lies you know how it is, you students like us?" I had to stop for breath and with a question otherwise I would have rambled on

incessantly. I could feel the embarrassment pouring out of me and could do nothing to stop it – fortunately the need to pause for breath came to my rescue.

"Passports!!" the crone behind the desk was getting impatient.

"Oh oui, naturellement," I attempted an air of cool disregard and quickly fished my passport back out of my rucksack and together with Danny's, who had remained mute behind me, handed them over to the crone. She snatched them out of my hand, glanced momentarily at them before handing them back with a garbled muttering and finger pointing back out of the office door.

"She says to follow the road round to the left and to put your tent under the trees where you will see other small tents pitched," explained Adonis, he had a marked American accent, "hi, by the way, I'm Brad and you are?"

I took his out-stretched hand and winced under the friendly but clearly 'she's mine' hand-shake. "Hi, I'm Marty and this is Dan," Marty and Dan sounded so much better than Martin and Danny and I felt the, almost urgent, need to come across as a man of the world rather than how I felt, a silly pubescent schoolboy. "We're heading around the country, taking in some of the sights and culture." I knew it sounded naff and, with every garbled utterance coming out of my mouth, I was digging myself into a deeper hole which, if I wasn't careful, I would struggle to get out of.

"Have you come far today?"

"Yeah, well we made it outta Cherbourg pretty easy. Bin on the road mosta the day and kinda figure we'd better find somewhere to kip down for the night. See what tomorrow brings – may stay on for a couple of days see what the town has to offer." I thought I sounded cool but the wry smile across Brad's face made me feel uncomfortable – had he noticed? Of course, he had and what was worse, Marie-France was now hanging on to his arm which, if nothing else, confirmed that any chance I may have thought I had was rapidly going up in smoke.

"Tell you what Marty," said Brad, "why don't you and Dan here get yourselves sorted out and we'll catch up with you later, take you into the town, show you around – think you might like it. Plenty of available French ladies around for a couple of young lads to admire." He winked and made a soft punch against my shoulder. I winced feeling how I'd like to punch his lights out.

"Yeah that sounds groovy," I nodded in a cool dude sort of way, "should be cool eh Dan?" I stared intently at my not so cool mate who had turned away and was staring blankly out of the window.

"What? Yeah cool, whatever mate," he gave me a bored look, "where we gonna pitch the tent I feel knackered, need a kip."

I turned back to my new friends and raised my eyes skyward, "give us a couple of hours, yeah, and we'll meet you back here, is that ok?"

"That'll be fine," smiled Brad, he glanced down at his watch, "it's just before six now, let's say we meet back here at eight thirty. That should give Danny-boy here enough time for some much-needed beauty sleep," he smirked and punched Danny in a playfully, bullying 'I'm the big cheese' sort of way.

Danny scowled at Brad, it was obvious that there was no love lost between the two of them. Clearly things had not got off to a good start which, given that we had literally, only just met seemed to me to be a bit odd. But I wanted to play it down, hoping that time would sort things out. Acting as spokesman I agreed that we would be ready in a couple of hours.

We hefted our rucksacks back over our shoulders and, without a backward glance, headed out the door.

"Fucking wanker!" spat Dan as soon as he was out of earshot, "who the fuck does he think he is?"

"I think he was just protecting his territory," I suggested, "Did you see his girlfriend, Marie-France, she was something else. I reckon if he hadn't been there she would've come on to me."

"Yeah right," scoffed Dan, "she would've had you for breakfast and spat you out given all your experience with women," he laughed, the memory of the earlier piss-take from Brad already fading, "come on let's find somewhere to pitch up. If I can't get any kip I need something to eat, I'm starving."

****

"Why do you 'ave to act so big-'eaded?" hissed Marie-France, "those boys adn't done anyting to make you be'ave the way you did, they were just being friendly and a little shy. I tought they were nice."

"Nuts", replied Brad, he could feel his hackles rise, if there was one thing he didn't like it was being criticised especially if was coming from a girl, if you please!

"Those guys were just a couple of limey losers – need a few lessons in growing up. Think I'll show them how it's done later-on." He laughed condescendingly at his supposedly naïve girlfriend, "c'mon, loosen up it'll be fun."

"Not if I've got anything to do with it," Marie-France replied haughtily and turned and walked out of the office.

****

We had found a small spot to pitch our tent, it seemed to be ok although the flies buzzing about in the small marshy area just a few yards away did make me wonder if we had done the right thing. But now all I wanted to do was get out, go into town and start to have fun.

"C'mon mate for Pete's sake, or we'll miss them," I twisted my watch round for Danny to see, "we agreed eight thirty and I don't want to miss this evening." I nudged Danny again.

Clearly, he was reluctant to go and mumbled into his pillow of assorted clothes he had extracted from his rucksack

"Nah I don't fancy it, I'm tired, need to get some sleep. You go, tell me in the morning how you get on".

"Suit yourself," I grumbled, "hope this isn't how it's gonna be for the whole trip. Just remember we're in it together. This is our chance to let them know back home that we can do it."

I did my best to convince Danny to get up and come with me but he was having none of it so I chucked in the towel and crawled out of the tent. Although it was almost half eight and the sun was slowly descending into the sea it was still warm and I could feel my shirt sticking to my back as I half ran, half walked through the camp site back to the reception where Brad and Marie-France were waiting.

"Hey man, where's your buddy, all tucked up in his bed already? Poor sweet little fella." Brad winked at me, failing to disguise his sarcasm.

"He's not feeling too good, he's been sick." I wasn't in the mood for making excuses for Danny but at the same time I wasn't going to let this Yankee bull-shitter get one over on me. The more I got to know him the less I was beginning to like him. "Hi Marie-France!" I turned my attention towards the new love of my life and in return I was rewarded with pecks on both cheeks – I almost swooned at the touch of her lips as they softly caressed my skin.

"Ello Marty. Never mind your friend will feel better in the morning once 'e 'as 'ad a good sleep and then per'aps we can all go out again. Maybe I will invite my friend Nicole next time."

So, she has a friend here too I thought. If she's anywhere near as lovely as M-F then this is going to be the making of a great holiday. But then there's Brad – every silver lining has its cloud.

The walk into town took us down through a pine wood which opened out onto a small, deserted beach. The sea looked to be far away in the distance and the beach was dotted with what looked like wooden sheds suspended on stilts about fifteen feet high above the rocky shoreline. I was fascinated, "What are they?" I asked.

Brad just shrugged his shoulders, "Search me buddy, some sort of French idea of a house I guess. These Frenchie's have got some really weird ideas."

I watched Marie-France's reaction to this barely disguised insult. She took a deep breath and chewed frantically on her bottom lip. Clearly this arsehole was starting to get on her nerves I thought hopefully.

"That's not fair Bradley please don't make jokes about 'ow people make their living in my country. They are 'onest and 'ard working, more than can be said for you!" There was a barely disguised spite in her voice. She turned her back on him and smiled at me, "they are used by those fishermen in the town that don't 'ave boats, it means they can still catch fish without going out to sea. But it means that it is only when the tide is in and they 'ave to wait until it goes out again before they can go 'ome."

"Don't call me Bradley again, do you hear," Brad snapped, his face a deep shade of puce – it was almost scary how quickly his behaviour had changed, this bloke was clearly someone who didn't like the idea of being seen to be anything other than a perfect Peter – reminded me of Frank's dad!

Anyhow I felt that I had the measure of this pillock (cos that's what I now thought of him and all in a couple of minutes too) so I decided to jump in and ignore his little tantrum completely. "That's interesting Marie-France, that sounds like a clever idea to me." I stole a furtive glance at Brad just in time to see him raise his eyes sky-wards with an air of complete frustration at my obvious stupidity. But I wasn't going to be put off by anything he could throw at me – he had shown his hand and betrayed his weakness – he was jealous, and I could tell that this was made worse by the fact that the gorgeous girl who he felt he had won could also see through his thin veneer of perfection. So, with the right amount of encouragement from yours truly, could be prised out of his arms. I was feeling upbeat – I was on a roll.

As we rounded a point on the beach I caught my first glimpse of Fouras town itself. A sea wall separated the town from the beach where gaily coloured tents had been erected I guessed where people modestly changed before racing down to plunge into the sea. The old town rose up gently from the sea wall and even from the point on the bay I could make out the flags draped outside the buildings, fluttering in the gentle breeze. The town was ablaze with lights and colour, and I could hear the sound of a band playing somewhere in the distance.

"Oh! wow this is fantastic," I exclaimed, I allowed my boyish enthusiasm to get the better of me and quickened my pace. To my delight Marie-France came up alongside me and we headed off, side-by-side, leaving a still-sulking Brad a little further behind. Eventually he caught us up and together we climbed up the steps from the beach and took in the sight that met us – I was aghast.

Everywhere I looked there were crowds of people milling around – brightly covered market stalls selling everything from beach wear, sandals, food of all descriptions – things I had never even knew existed were attacking each of my senses and exploding inside my head. The noise of music, fun and laughter was everywhere. I momentarily forgot all about Brad and turned and put my hand on Marie-France shoulder. "This is unbelievable what is it all for?" I had to shout in her ear to make myself heard.

"Do you not know what day it is?" she shouted back, I shook my head, "It's Bastille Day our French national holiday," she smiled at me indulgently, "it's the day the French people began our escape from the tyranny of the aristocracy – it's a great day." She seemed to blow the last few words gently in my ear and I found myself falling ever further under her spell – I think I was falling in love, no damnit I was in love!

I looked across to where Brad was standing on the other side of her – he was clearly not enjoying the evening and I began to see him for what I thought he really was. A spoilt little rich American boy sent over to Europe by an over-indulgent father who was chairman of a big company (probably making Barbie dolls, or something similar) who wanted his son to see how much better he was than the peasants on the other side of the pond. My mind was working nineteen to the dozen and I was enjoying every minute of it. I was going to get the better of the bastard regardless of what it took.

And then something happened.

"Allo mister Marty, 'ow are you?" There in front of me stood Bernard, looking cool and chic in tight bell-bottoms, flowery shirt and neck-tie staring intently at Marie-France with an unmistakeable hungry look etched across his face. "Are you not going to introduce me to your friend Marty?" – how could someone talk to me when as far as he was concerned I wasn't even there??

"Err, oh, high, yeah, erm, Bernard, this is Marie-France and this is her, er, boyfriend Brad, he's an American" I added that last bit as I remembered dad saying that, generally, the Yanks and French couldn't stand each other. My mind was working overtime but then, what a stroke of genius I thought, let Brad sort out this interfering Frenchman. After all, as far as he was concerned everyone in Europe (and especially the French) were peasants. I was just going to stand by and let these two, rivals for the romantic attentions of the delightful Mademoiselle Marie-France sort out their obvious differences.

Brad scowled at Bernard and muttered a gruff "Hi", putting his arm protectively around M-F's shoulder as he did so. The message was obvious – hands off she's mine. Clearly, he saw Bernard as a potential threat whereas I was just seen as a minor irritant which, as far as I was concerned, could only work in my favour. It meant I would be under Brad's radar while he fought a frontal assault against, what he probably thought was, the greater threat from the smooth-talking Bernard. I couldn't help but notice how she had winced as Brad had pulled her towards him.

Despite the heady, party atmosphere in the pretty streets of the town nobody could have failed to notice the animosity between the two B's that had gone from zero to a hundred miles an hour in fractions of a second. I stole a secret smile at Marie-France who had wrested herself from Brad's arm and had come over to stand next to me.

Bernard fired off a stream of unintelligible French at Marie-France and she responded equally rapidly and, I have to say, sounded rather upset into the bargain.

"For fucks sake, speak fucking English can't you!" stormed Brad. His face was turning a deep shade of puce with every second that passed and, hey, not a single word had passed between the two antagonists.

"Eh Yank, don't speak to 'er like that," replied Bernard, his eyes blazing, "I was jus' askin' Marie-France where she was from and 'ow long she 'ad been in Fouras. Don' worry I won't steal 'er from you. Although it wouldn't be difficult if I wanted to."

Brad bristled at Bernard's response but chose to keep his mouth shut, although I could have sworn I heard him mutter "fuckin' frog" under his breath.

Bernard turned to me winked and whispered, "I also asked her what she is doin' with that idiot when there's an 'andsome English man standing next to her." He laughed gently and patted me on the shoulder. "Don' worry I 'ave a beautiful girlfriend who should be 'ere in a short while. Stay around and you can meet 'er."

I nodded my thanks and turned to watch Marie-France who had pulled Brad to one side and was talking heatedly to him. He stood there with his head hung down and I couldn't fail to notice how she pushed him away when he tried to rest his hands on her shoulder. This was working out better than I had planned – they seemed to be on the verge of breaking up, I decided to step in.

"Hey, you two, are you coming with me and Bernard? He's invited us over to that bar just across the street." Brad gave a look of total disbelief at what I was suggesting but I couldn't help but notice Marie-France smile at the idea.

"Why would we want to spend any time with that frog wanker," muttered Brad half under his breath but not so low that M-F couldn't fail but hear.

"If that's 'ow you feel Bradley," - I couldn't help but notice the sarcastic tone in Marie-France's voice – "then per'aps you should go," She turned and headed across the street to where Bernard and I were standing, "c'mon let's go meet your friends."

I glanced back across where Brad was still standing, mouth agape, then he turned on his heel and pushed his way roughly between the startled crowd who had witnessed his outburst. I flashed a brief smile at the onlookers, trying to look sympathetic at the events but inside I felt smug and, not a little, victorious – my presumed nemesis had been defeated simply down to his own self-importance and brashness. I seemed to me that he would have been more sensible to allow people to think he was an idiot, rather than open his mouth and prove it. Anyway, as far as I was concerned the bastard deserved everything that had happened. We headed across the road, Marie-France had slipped her arm through mine and I felt like a million dollars. I desperately wanted to turn around and flash a self-satisfied smirk in Brad's direction but, for one I didn't want to come across as a victor even though that's how I felt and, secondly, I was worried that he may still be looking over and decide to follow us and even have a go at me. I'm a lover not a fighter – it sounded better than coward!!

The town was buzzing people, young and old, all smiles and laughter – it was one big party. I couldn't understand why it was all going on, I turned to Marie-France, "what's happening here, what's this all about, is this a party or something?" I had to get close to her ear to make myself heard, but I felt intoxicated by the sweet smell of her hair and the closeness of her fabulous body.

She turned towards me our noses touching for a brief second, she smiled, "I 'ave already told you – it's Bastille Day, we all party on Bastille Day."

"Oh right, yeah, of course so you did. I've heard of it but don't know too much about it." I gave her a weak shrug. Truth was how could I remember much about anything other than her!!

"I'll tell you more about it," she replied, "but not now, let's 'ave some fun." She grabbed hold of my hand and dragged me through the crowd, heading through the open door of bar where I could see Bernard embracing a gorgeous blonde.

Bernard was not wrong, his girlfriend, Natalie, was gorgeous but I still couldn't believe my luck – Marie-France seemed to be all over me. I felt a little out of my depth they all seemed so much older than me but somehow seemed to have me as the centre of their attention. "You are so brave," Natalie almost gushed, "to come over to our country on you own. Bernard tell me you are with a friend and are travelling with your thumb?" she gave me the thumbs up, "I do not think mes parents would let me do that, what if you meet nasty people?"

"Ah oh well, we know how to look after ourselves and I am a judo black belt," I lied. I was bold-over by her accent and, took a sip of my second glass of French biere. It was going to my head - before this dad had only ever let me drink shandy. But, with the attention I was getting, particularly from Marie-France I felt like I was on cloud nine and loving it. I took a glance at Bernard and he winked at me over the rim of his glass, I think he was enjoying it as much as I was – or was he laughing at me? I wasn't sure. Whatever it was I quickly realised that, if I wasn't careful, I would make an arse of myself and I tried to make light of Natalie's questioning and concentrate on things going on around me. But, with Marie-France drawing herself ever closer to me – blimey, somehow, she had managed to weave her legs around mine and by now was sitting half-on my lap.

I looked up at the bright orb of the moon and a shiver ran across my whole body. It took a few brief seconds to realise where I was and then I felt the reassuring warmth of Marie-France lying close next to me. I glanced at my watch, 'blimey', I thought it's nearly one-thirty, way past my bedtime. But then I closed my eyes against the moons glow – there was nothing I could do about it right at that moment

The remainder of the evening had been a blur, but I couldn't fail to realise that Marie-France and I were making our way along the promenade. It had lost many of the earlier party-goers. We came across a flight of rough, rocky steps which took us down onto the beach where we strolled along arm in arm across the sand. She kicked off her sandals and gathered them up into her free hand, I did the same, stooping to un-tie the laces of my plimsols and removing my socks which I stuffed inside them, before tying the laces together and slinging them coolly over my shoulder.,

Tall and tanned and young and handsome
The boy from Ipanema goes walking
And when he passes each girl he passes goes ahhhh.

Marie-France stopped mid-stride and turned to face me. "You know Marty I think you are a very 'andsome boy." - 'Here comes the big but', - I thought through my semi-alcoholic haze, 'this is where you get the brush off'- "An I like you very much, very very much." -could I be hearing this right?

She grabbed my face in both hands and pulled me towards her. I felt her lips brushing against mine and then the grind of teeth against teeth as she pushed against my mouth with a kind of chomping motion, trying to open my mouth. Immediately her tongue pushed in, furtively searching out my tongue. I had never been kissed like this by a girl before – who was I kidding, I'd never been kissed by a girl before except when I was about nine at junior school during a game of kiss-chase!!

I desperately tried to remember whether I had cleaned my teeth and then gave up worrying as she seemed to pull me off my feet and I found myself on my back with her on top of me – what happened to my black-belt judo skills I thought – did I care?

What followed, as far as my alcoholic haze can remember, was a desperate struggling and, on my part, loud groaning as this French vixen worked her magic on all my senses. As Marie-France concentrated on trying to encircle my tonsils with her tongue I found my hand had disappeared under her tee-shirt, slowly working its way upwards. I stopped suddenly as my furtively searching fingers came into contact with the elastic straps of her bra. I didn't know what to do next, she didn't seem to have noticed – her mind was clearly on other things. But, what if I moved my hand further to the right groping for the hook, what if I unhooked it? Further-more what if I did unhook it, what the hell would I do then?

I was sobering up quickly and was quickly realising that I was well out of my depth, swirling into the whirlpool of self-doubt. Suddenly relief came in the form of the previous hours spent in the bar with Bernard and his girlfriend – Marie-France froze, intoxication had over-taken her and, as quickly as she had started devouring me, she stopped, her eyes closed, and she fell into a deep slumber. Was I relieved? – well I guess it was difficult for me to say. Here I was on a strange beach, in a strange town, in a strange country with a, relatively, strange beauty lying half on top of me snoring gently, having almost taken me to a level I had only dreamed of in the security of my own bedroom. Well I did what any young Romeo would do, I lay there, a feeling of self-satisfaction washing over me – without realising it I had taken my first tentative steps into becoming a man.

I opened my eyes a second time – one-thirty-five – and then with a start I felt water swirl around my feet and soaked the bottom of my jeans – the tide was coming in!!

"Quick get up," I struggled to move the sleeping form lying across me as another wavelet poured just a little bit higher, "come on wake up before we drown!" My urgent ministrations had the right effect as Marie-France woke and leapt up in one smooth single moment – suddenly sober with no apparent memory of the previous few hours.

"Merde!" she exclaimed, "quelle heure est il?" – I think she had forgotten I was English.

"Une heure et demi," I replied, putting on my best schoolboy-franglais, "I think we had better be getting back," resorting to my trusted native tongue.

"Oh merde, ma tante, mon oncle!!" Marie-France continued to moan as she pulled on her sandals, while I struggled with my plimsols, only realising at the last minute that my socks were stuffed into the toes, "we must be quick my aunt will be worried et mon oncle, 'e will be verrr verrrrr angry with me."

I put a comforting hand on M-F's arm and it seemed to do the trick and calm her down at little. I felt that I had to reassure her that I would go with her, even though I didn't have a clue where she lived or whether I would even be able to find my way back to the camp-site afterwards.

We held hands as we walked back along the sandy beach, gradually leaving the lights of the little town behind us, guided only by the light of the moon. Marie-France grew calmer and I learned a little more about her. She was eighteen (eighteen! I couldn't believe I had scored with an eighteen-year old!) and lived with her parents in a small town not too far from Paris. Her aunt and uncle had invited her to spend some of her holiday with them in Fouras and she was expecting her parents to join her there in a couple of weeks.

I was keen or, at least I think I was keen, to discover how Brad fitted into this picture – I just knew he had a bigger role to play in this story than I wanted him to have, But, I wasn't to be disappointed as, apparently she had met him only a couple of days earlier in the town and he had been all over her like a rash and she was not sorry to see the back of him – I could feel the elation growing!! He was on a tour of Europe with his parents – his father being something in the American embassy in Brussels about which Brad would brag given the slightest opportunity.

Her aunt and uncle had encountered Brad and his family in the town and thought it would be a good idea if their niece were to show him around. 'Thanks for that,' she had muttered under her breath, in French of course, and was thus lumbered with this guy whose ego, she thought, was bigger than the Titanic – I loved the analogy, remembering what had happened to that great ship now lying several hundred feet down somewhere in the Atlantic.

We continued, on past the entrance to my camp-site and I was relieved to find that Marie-France was staying less than half a mile away further on. As we approached the house I could see it was in total darkness. I walked with her as far as the gate where she turned and held out her hand – I thought she was going to shake mine and was a little surprised given that just a couple of hours earlier she had been trying to devour me! But I needn't have worried she pulled me towards her and planted a deep throaty kiss before slowly pulling away. "Can we meet tomorrow Marty?" she breathed softly in my ear, "an' I will bring my friend Nicole with me an' could can bring your friend too, that would be fun yes?"

"Yeah that would be great," I replied, thinking that if tomorrow was anything like the evening I had just had how could it not be fun?"

"We will meet you in the town by the steps next to the beach then at twelve. Don't be late Marty."
And she was gone up the steps and through the front-door. I stood there transfixed until I saw a light come on in an upstairs window and there she was standing at the window waving down to me and blowing a kiss. Wow what a start to my big adventure, midday couldn't come quickly enough!
"I met this bloke last evening, he's in a tent just over there," Danny, still in his sleeping bag, head rested awkwardly on a combination of folded jeans and rucksack gazed up at me, doubtless not ready to hear about my evening in case he regretted not coming. "Says he's going to be around this dump for a few days and then heading off somewhere else, wants to know if we fancy hitching up with him, what d'you reckon?"
How the hell are three of us going to be able to get a lift?" I objected, "didn't you think about that?" I could feel my hackles rise, sometimes, I thought, Danny just didn't seem to get it.
"No, idiot! The blokes got a car, an old Jowett Javelin, looks a bit of a wreck but it goes. He's touring around France for a couple of weeks before he heads back to Lyon where he works. Said he's going back along the Loire Valley and wondered if we were interested."

It was obvious Danny was keen not to have to spend hours by the roadside waiting for lifts and, in some ways, I could see where he was coming from. But, right now I was caught in a bit of a dilemma – easy lift or the chance to score with the delightful mademoiselle Marie-France. I suddenly realised I didn't know her surname!

I decided to appeal to his male ego. "You should've come last evening it was good," I began, "we….."
He interrupted, "Yeah, right, I bet Brad was just a bundle of laughs. I'm sure you heard his bloody life story, big-headed American arsehole."
"Marie-France dumped him no sooner than we got into town. Not only that but guess who she's taken a liking too?" I put on my best cool dude image, vainly attempting to do the one-eyebrow lift so favoured by Simon Templar. "And," I added before he could interrupt, "we've arranged to meet later today and she's bringing along a mate just for you Danny, my son!"
I knew that appealing to Danny's, often self-inflated, ego would do the trick. "What's her name, what does she look like?" I could almost hear him slavering.
"Hang on, hang on, I haven't met her. If you want to come along then you can find out for yourself. What do you say?"

"Yeah why not. But what are we going to do about this bloke Wilcox and the chance of a lift?"

"Well let's see how today goes and then we can make our minds up then. Fair?" I wasn't too keen to give up my chances with Marie-France just yet but, at the same time, I could also see where Danny was coming from and, after all, this was our first time away from home on our own. We were the pathfinders for those who were to follow in our footsteps. We were explorers and we both knew that we would milk our tales of derring-do for all it was worth when we returned home.

Later that morning having eaten a delightful meal of pork luncheon meat and slightly sloppy instant mashed potato I found my way to the, less than clean, toilet block and dived under a tepid shower. I wanted to look (and smell) my best for the afternoon's encounter. Danny also, made an effort to tidy himself up and so just before midday we set off to make the acquaintance with les belle mademoiselles de Fouras.

We were not to be disappointed, Marie-France looked even more stunning than she had the previous day and Nicole, her friend, while she was slightly shorter was no less beautiful and I could tell that Danny was, thankfully, impressed.

The girls suggested that we walk along the promenade and into a small amusement arcade where they said the locals gathered to sit around, smoke and play the occasional game of table football. The arcade, while it was busy wasn't crowded and we bought four bottles of coke (alcohol was banned here) and asked for a few coins for the football machine.

The afternoon passed too quickly and a little before five the girls announced that they would have to return home for dinner but assured us that they would meet us outside the arcade just before eight that evening. I didn't have to ask Danny if he was happy about the arrangements, he was awestruck by Nicole and only too pleased to wait for a couple of hours to be able to meet up with her again.

"I think I may have scored with Nicole, Marty," he bragged, "did you see the way she was running her hand over my thigh?" I tell you what she is one hell of a little French lady."

Truth was I had watched them and felt a little jealous because, although Marie-France had kept close to me I sensed an air of remoteness about her. But she had held tightly onto my arm just before they had left us, almost as though she didn't want me to go. The thing was I was a little confused as to how the coming evening would go, was I going to be hit by a 'thanks but no thanks' bombshell? While I didn't want to admit it, my naivety was beginning to make its presence felt. We wandered back to our tent which even after only one night was looking worse than a mess. It was obvious that I wouldn't be asking Marie-France if she wanted to come back to my place to see my etchings! We struggled through a re-constituted dish of chicken curry and rice, learning very rapidly that half-cooked dehydrated peas tasted worse than chewing through a beach pebble. But, beggars can't be choosers and, by the time we had been to the communal service block to wash our cooking equipment and plates, it was time to head back into town.

It was a glorious evening with little breeze and the waves lapping lazily against the shore. I had taken off my shoes and socks and was luxuriating in the sand filtering through between my toes.

"This is the life eh Danny," I mused, feeling the freedom of being in a foreign country with no day to day pressures of school or the constant, irritating gibes from mum telling to do this and do that. I was at peace with myself and had the prospect of who knows what in the coming few hours.

"Yeah," replied Dan, his mind clearly on other, more carnal, thoughts, "hope Nicole's not changed outta that tight little t-shirt. It showed off her tits a treat."

"God he's a bloody moron," I thought to myself, "got no class whatsoever – think I'll have to find someone more adult to come with me next year." His less than sophisticated comments had dragged me out of my own highly sophisticated reverie. I felt in my pocket and pulled out a half-crushed packet of Gauloises and a book of matches that I had forgotten I had bought the previous evening. "Wanna smoke?" I asked.

"Yeah why not, these are bloody good." Replied Danny holding out his hand expectantly. I recalled my experience the last time I had tried one in the back of the old van and was determined not to let the strength of this decidedly French pastime get the better of me again. I struck a match and Danny leaned forward to take his first drag, the smoke obviously took him by surprised as he sucked in greedily and he began a fit of coughing which he was unable to control – I was sneakily pleased. I lit my own cigarette and, taking note of the effect, a deep drag had on Danny, just sucked in a little, blowing the smoke out through mouth and nostrils quickly, almost before it had a chance to reap its effects on me. I made it – no coughing, no dizziness,

I had learned the secret of how to smoke a Gauloise and maintain a cool outer demeanour which would be the envy of all my mates at school – if, of course, I took any back home with me.

The girls were waiting for us when we arrived along the beach and they both looked stunning. Marie-France came straight up to me and planted the biggest kiss, full on the lips, that had my mind swirling. Danny mad a grab for Nicole and I couldn't help but notice that she seemed to recoil from his amorous advance. But, what the hell that was his problem, I was in seventh heaven and had no intention of letting his problems spoil my evening – friendship only stretched so far, especially if there was a beautiful girl waiting in the wings!

We wandered into the same bar we had found ourselves in the previous evening and I could feel my chest expanding as I took in the admiring glances from the assembled crowd as they looked at both girls admiringly as we walked past. We found a table tucked away in the far corner and, having seated the girls (and Danny) comfortably I announced that I would buy a round of drinks. "Ok what would you all like to drink?" I asked. "Beer, biere," was the chorused response and I quickly turned and made my way to the bar.

I caught the eye of the bar-tender, who strolled toward me, looking me up and down. "Please don't ask my age." I muttered quietly to myself.

"Qui monsieur, que voulez vous?" he almost seemed to be demanding a reply as to why I was there, not what I would like to drink.

I suddenly began to feel out of my depth and I looked past his shoulder into the mirror behind the bar. "Oh shit!" I almost shouted it out loud. There through the door walked Brad with a couple of other blokes who seemed to be his friends! I suddenly wanted to disappear down behind the nearest table. But too late, it was almost as if his eyes were drawn towards me and he pulled up short. The two goons behind him didn't stop in time and rammed straight into his back pushing him forward straight into a table occupied by two of the largest Frenchmen I have seen in my life. Drinks flew everywhere and the screech of chairs scraping backwards as the two man-mountains rose to their full height spitting out expletives which I would have loved to be able to translate.

"Oui monsieur!! The barman clearly was getting impatient with me and didn't seem to be at all interested in what was going happening on the other side of the room, "do you wan' un drink?"

"Ahh ... yeah, oui, err... four .... no sorry, quatre bieres si'l vous plait." I replied, my attention was focussed on Brad and his two new French buddies – all interest in the reason for being at the bar had evaporated.

Suddenly he was standing beside me, "See what you made me do arsehole," he hissed at me, "you've just cost me four francs to buy those two French wankers a drink." He had clearly lost none of his dislike for the male members of the Gallic race!

"Nothing to do with me mate, you should have been looking where you were going," I replied testily. Crikey! Where had that come from? I half expected a punch in the mouth as a response, perhaps a slap around the chops but, nothing, he just stood there his face a deep shade of puce.

"Bar-keep! Two large beers for our froggie-friends over there and a bottle of red and three glasses!" he almost spat out his order only to be totally ignored by the bar tender who casually poured out the last of my four beers.

"Thank you, monsieur, dat will be trois francs if you please. Do you wanna tray monsieur?" It was obvious to me that the bar tender knew exactly what had taken place across the other side of the bar and was doing his utmost to make Brad and his cronies unwelcome.

"Please monsieur you will wait until I have finished serving zis young gentleman," he gave Brad a tolerant smile, baring a row of even white teeth, "thank you, monsieur," as I handed him the exact change, "enjoy your evening." I felt as though I had made a new friend and ally.

I carried the drinks back to our table, "Did you see what happened over there?" I said as I sat down. "Brad kicked up a bit of a scene at the bar I don't think he's happy about forking out for drinks for those two guys and seeing us in here." I hoped that I didn't sound as worried as I was beginning to feel.

"Please just ignore 'im," replied Marie-France, "'e always gets angry if 'e doesn't get 'is own way and then 'e thing 'e can boss people around. But 'e is a coward, 'e makes a big noise but runs away if someone says no."

"I hope she's right," I was thinking. "Well let's try not to let him spoil our evening," I said, "cheers everyone," and took a swig of my beer, not waiting for anyone to reply. "So, what shall we do?" I said as I clanked my half-empty glass down on the table – suddenly I didn't want to be in this bar a minute longer, I just hope it didn't show.

"Well I was planning on having a quiet drink for starters," replied Danny, he turned and smiled at Nicole, "and then maybe a romantic stroll along the beach eh?" Let's hope your antics at the bar haven't put the kybosh on that Marty."

He was lucky and so was I. Brad and his two cronies had not stayed around too long, having quickly finished their drinks before pushing their way back out of the now crowded bar, casting malevolent eyes in our direction as they did so.

We remained in the bar for a while longer primarily to allow time for Brad to get well clear of the area and also because Danny dipped into his notoriously tight pocket and offered to buy a second round. We found this lifted the atmosphere between us and we agreed to go our separate ways with our respective escorts then meet up a bit later.

"What are you doing Marty," said Marie-France. I couldn't help looking both ways as we left the bar just to check to see if Brad was hanging around somewhere.

"Oh nothing, I was just wondering where we could go to be alone," I lied deftly squeezing her hand and kissing her ear, "or do you already know somewhere?"

"Oh, I think I know just the place where we can be alone," she almost whispered and returned my kiss, "come, let us go this way." She laughed and started to skip down the road pulling me along with her.

We ran along the crowded promenade, racing past people, laughing merrily as we went. I could see them watching us, curious as to what we were doing, I also heard others wolf whistling and laughing as we ran past. Was this what love was like? If so give me more of it. I was falling madly and hopelessly in love with this adorable girl and I was certain she felt the same. How could this have happened in less than two days?

The further away from the town that we walked, the quieter and darker became the promenade with the lights stretching further apart. We passed another couple as we slowed to a leisurely walk. I pulled her closer and put my arm around her shoulder and she rested her head on my shoulder.

"Let's go down these steps," she whispered, "we can walkalong the sand, there are some rocks just around the corner where we can rest."

I needed no second bidding and we quickly headed down the steps onto the beach. I could see where she meant for us to go and within a few short minutes we were sitting side by side on a low rock.

Marie-France pulled my arm towards her and rested. She reached into her bag and pulled out a biro. "This is my address Marty," she said as she wrote on my upper arm, "I know you are 'ere only for a few days and when you 'ave left I want you to write to me every day, you will won't you?"

"Of course, I will," I replied, "and I'll give you my address too, but not on your arm, give me a piece of paper or something."

She shuffled about in her bag and brought out a small card which she handed to me. I quickly scratched down my address and slipped the card and biro back into her bag, at the same time I pulled her closer to me and kissed her full on the mouth, allowing my tongue to trace across her teeth waiting for her to invite me in. She responded immediately and parted her lips further, her own tongue darted in and out of my mouth.

"Come let's lie down 'ere." She whispered and pulled me towards a dry patch of sand hidden away from any prying eyes. I needed no second bidding!

She pushed her breast upwards into my chest as we lay, so close to each-other. The moon cast a long shadow across the flat calm of the sea, with barely a ripple as the wavelets advanced slowly up the beach towards us.

I turned my face into the soft warmth of her neck and she arched her head back, allowing me to brush my lips tenderly across her throat and my tongue traced light circles underneath her ears.

My hands traced slowly over the soft contours of her belly and I allowed the tips of my fingers to dip inquisitively under the top hem of her shorts – slowly allowing them to move just a little lower with each tender stroke. I could feel her breathing getting more urgent and she began to quiver under my soft touch – my loins ached with desire. I felt the soft elastic of her pants and I pushed slightly lower, stopping as my finger-tips came into contact with the beginnings of a soft forest.

"Oooohh Maaaarteeee……ooooohhhhhh," she sighed, her words barely sounding above the slow lapping of the waves, "do you 'ave eneeee protecshuuun?"

I was momentarily stumped. My hands quickly moved back upwards, had she seen Brad? I looked around in case he and his mates were advancing on us. "Well I've got my old boy scout pen-knife in my pocket, if that's any good." I replied, feeling the tightness in my trouser-area easing slightly.

"No silly," she gave a slightly forced giggle, "I don' wan' a babeee."

"Ah right, ok, I see what you mean," I said, momentarily stumped, "you mean a johnny-bag!" Truth was I'd never seen one up close, except the occasional discarded one in our local park - had never been brave enough to ask for one in the chemist - In fact I don't reckon I'd know what to do with one anyhow.

My trouser-area was now completely free, and I was left with a damp feeling around my groin area – damn that would mean a change of pants in the morning! "Oh no," I mumbled, "I didn't think you were ready to make love to me so soon," I was scrambling around for any excuse I could think of. My mind was desperately thinking of how I could get myself out of this one without making me look even more of a childish idiot than I felt at the moment. "I promise that I will buy some protection in the morning, honest." What more could I say, she seemed very disappointed and smiled at me sadly.

"You do promise me don't you Marty, tomorrow?"

"Yes, I really do promise," I said, and kissed her deeply to seal the deal, "so what would you like to do now – crikey, that sounded so stupid but, in some ways that was how I felt.

"Oh, let's just lie here for a while," she said, "I don't want to leave here yet," she returned my kiss and then sighed deeply as she lay with her head resting on my chest.

****

I kissed Marie-France at the gate of her home with a promise of meeting her the following afternoon.

We had remained on the beach for what seemed a long while but, in truth, was probably no more than an hour as I felt the fire had gone out slightly. We had wandered down to the shore and allowed the warm sea to wash over our feet. I had splashed Marie-France and she had reacted rather more differently to what I had expected and had covered my head and chest in water. I had decided not to retaliate and had then suggested that I walk her home.

I gave a final wave just before I rounded the corner and received a blown kiss in reply. Now where should I go? I checked my watch, two-thirty – blimey I didn't realise it was that late! I decided to walk back into the town and see if I could find Danny, in any event it was on my way back to the campsite.

The town was almost deserted with hardly no more than half a dozen couples wandering round and I saw one bar with music blaring almost to itself – I decided not to investigate further.

I found Danny sitting on a bench on the promenade looking very dejected. Oh dear it looked like things hadn't gone too well for Mr Mickelburgh. I sat myself down next to him.

"Alright mate, how did it go?"

"Don't fucking ask, what a waste of fucking time. Can't see any point of hanging around this dump anymore." Well that was telling things as they were. This was going to be a difficult conversation.

"What happened then, I thought you two were getting on really well."

"What happened was that she just wasn't up for it. We went along the beach, found a nice shady spot and then she just wanted to sit and talk. I tried my best, believe me I really tried!! But after a while I couldn't see the point of trying any more, I was getting nowhere – frigid old cow! See was telling me to piss off"

He was clearly upset that much was obvious. "So that's it I've had enough of this bloody place I think we need to get the hell outta here as soon as possible. If that bloke, whatisname, Wilcox is happy to take us with him then I think we should go."

I felt caught between a rock and a hard place. I knew we had jumped into this holiday together because we were good friends but, I had promised Marie-France that I would see her in the morning. But, was that being fair on Danny? We agreed from the start that we should stick together and that was one of the last things our parents had made us promise to do. I owed it to him so, with not a small amount of reluctance I agreed that perhaps we should speak to Wilcox in the morning.

"C'mon mate, lets head back," I said, "it'll be daylight if we don't make a move soon, I reckon we could do with getting our heads down."

I couldn't sleep; my mind was in turmoil. Marie-France had, in the two days I had known her, worked her way under my skin. And here I was walking away from someone who had declared her love for me. I must be mad, but this was my, no our, big adventure and my head told me I should support Danny and carry on as we had planned. I was still awake when the sky was gradually get brighter.

****

"C'mon mate wake up, it's nearly nine and Wilcox wants to know whether we're going with him!!"

Danny was shaking me roughly and I almost leapt up, suddenly wide awake. "What time d'you say?" I demanded.

"Nine!" he replied, "come on let's get moving."

Well that was it, the decision was made, we were leaving and there was nothing more I could do about it. I pulled on my clothes and crawled out of the tent. Danny was talking to Wilcox who was sitting outside his tent hands wrapped around a cup of coffee.

Wilcox raised himself up and walked over, hand outstretched, "Hi you must be Marty," we shook hands, "hope you're ok with our arrangements, I was telling Danny that I'm more than happy to take you two as far as Lyon, should be there in three days. I'm not needed back in work until early next week, so it will give us time to see a bit of the country. What do you say?"

"Yeah sounds good," I mumbled, "sorry I don't mean to sound grumpy, didn't sleep too well last night," I didn't want to give the bloke the impression that I wasn't grateful, "it'll be great, what sort of time did you want to head off?"

"Well as soon as we can to be honest. I want to get a few miles under my belt before it gets too busy in the town, we need to go through there to get on the road for Nantes. So, if you and Danny can get yourselves ready to go in around an hour, that would be great."

Going through the town, I thought, that might mean I may see Marie-France and perhaps I could get him to stop just for a second while I explain to her what's happening and that, come what may, I would see her again

We managed to pack our rucksacks in record time and broke down the tent, not caring too much about folding it down and packing into its bag. Wilcox said he had plenty of room in the boot of his car and it would hurt to leave the tent lose to allow the air to get into it as it was still a bit damp.

The old car bounced across the field and past the camp reception office. "Well I'm not sorry to see the back of this place," said Danny, he was sitting up front next to Wilcox.

"Didn't you like Fouras," he replied, "I thought it was quite a nice little town, a bit too noisy for my taste but I thought it would have been right up your street."

"Nah, not really," said Danny, "just think it was a mix of a grotty campsite and horrible people we met in the town."

"Is that how you feel Marty" asked Wilcox, turning around to me.

"No, it's not a bad place," I replied, "I quite like it, but we came over to see a bit of France and we haven't got all that long to be able to stay in one place."

"That sounds a bit philosophical," said Wilcox, "but I can see where you're coming from.

We were approaching the centre of the town and it was clear that it was getting busy, the pavements were already crowded. I looked this way and that for a glimpse of Marie-France, but I was fairly sure that it was a hopeless cause.

The car pulled up sharply as the traffic lights at the main crossroads turned to red. I turned around to look out of the back window and at that moment, no more than twenty yards behind us, both Marie-France and Nicole came walking around the corner. I quickly wound down the passenger door window and called out her name. She looked up and saw me waving, suddenly realising what was happening. She began to run towards the car, but Nicole grabbed her arm trying to pull her back. The car jerked forward as the lights turned to green and suddenly we were moving further away. I called again but she was disappearing into the distance. The car turned a corner and she disappeared from view.

I slumped back into the seat, "Shit," I muttered.

"Everything ok?" asked Wilcox, "do you need me to stop?"

"No, it's alright," interrupted Danny, "it's just a couple of girls we met last night. They'll get over us."

"Yeah, they'll get over us," I muttered under my breath, "but will I get over her?" I lay back against the seat and closed my eyes, there was nothing more to say or do. I determined to come back for her, maybe when we are heading back, I didn't know. I pulled up the sleeve of my shirt to read where she had written her address. it wasn't there!! It had been rubbed off – how was I ever going to be able to find her?

****

PART 2

More Fun in the Country

My head dropped back into the soft leather of the rear seat and I closed my eyes as Wilcox slowly manoeuvred the old car through the town traffic. I gazed out of the car window at the crowds of people ambling along, without a care in the world, enjoying the summer sun. I felt wretched, it wouldn't have taken much for me to cry I was feeling so bad. I was full of self-pity, feeling like I had let down myself and Marie-France - let's face it I had also missed out on popping my cherry and, you never know, but maybe hers too! She would never forgive me and who could blame her, let's face it I would never be able to explain myself and I could never expect her to want to ever see me again – I was just a lost cause.

The car ground to a halt, it looked like there was a hold-up just ahead, perhaps an accident I thought, and maybe a chance that we would stop just long enough for me to jump out and head back to find her. What would I say to her? The damage had been done, she had seen me driving away from her and, whatever I could say would not alter the fact that she would just look at me as a snivelling coward and who could blame her. But then my rational side jumped in and I knew that, however I may feel, it would not be fair on Danny. So, I resolved to just sit back, put my intrepid adventurers face back on and get on with life. What was I a man or a mouse? Yeah, I know what you're thinking – get out of the car boy and lose that cherry while you can!!

After a few short minutes the blockage, whatever it was, cleared and we found ourselves moving forward again and before very much longer the town traffic soon gave way to the open road. We were heading north, back towards La Rochelle and then on further to Nantes. The weather was hot with the sun beating down mercilessly and I was secretly glad that we were in the car. We were passing the endless fields, what looked like, withered bushes no more that two or three feet tall. My curiosity was pricked, "What's that, in the fields?" I asked.

"They're grape vines," came the reply, "this area is well known for producing some of the worlds' finest wines from those grapes, you ought to try it sometime. I think they may be picking the grapes a little further south already, it's much warmer down there and where the summer has been so good, it may mean we will be in for a bumper crop." he enthused.

It was clear that Wilcox considered himself a connoisseur of fine wines and I had obviously, however unintentionally, steered him onto his favourite subject, wine and the history thereof. I sat back and allowed the dirge to wash over me while I watched Danny, as the captive audience in the front seat, feign interest, occasionally half turning his head back to me with a lethal sneer spread across his face. I confess to taking some pleasure out of his suffering – such was our friendship!

My head banged sharply against the side-window as the car lurched from side to side. I quickly came to – I must have nodded off – as we ground to a halt.

"Bloody hell, what's gone wrong now?" mumbled Wilcox as he climbed out of the car. He wandered around to the front of the car, already I could see the perspiration collecting on his forehead (he was a bit like Bobby Charlton with a few wisps of hair combed across an otherwise bald pate). He mouthed a few obscenities and came around to Danny's side of the car and threw open the door, "C'mon lads out you get, you'll have to give me a hand, we've got a bloody puncture!"

We've got a puncture indeed! How did we come to have anything to do with his car and, besides I didn't have a clue about repairing a puncture, I smiled to myself as I pictured having a puncture in a johnny bag. I guessed I would be told to get out then in a slightly different sort of way – who was I kidding, I didn't have a bloody clue what I was talking about – it was all a pipe dream – the last few hours could have been so different!

Wilcox stomped off round to the back of the car and pulled open the boot lid. "Here give me a hand to get these bags out," he snorted, "they're yours after all." It was obvious that his otherwise chirpy disposition was clearly disappearing at a rapid rate of knots, I snuck a quick glance at Danny.

"What do you reckon?" I whispered.

"I've had enough of the bloke," replied my friend, "I'm bored to tears hearing about his bloody wine and then he started on about his job as a watch-maker. Bloody fascinating, I don't think. Oh, and thanks for nodding off in the back mate!"

That was his 'coup de gras' and sealed it for me. "Right then, let's clear off and leave him to it. If you're so pissed off, then we'll find our own way." I hadn't even bothered to look around to see where we were - and then I did. We were in the middle of nowhere, the road stretched out as far as the eye could see with just plain fields full of vines for company on either side. There was no sign of habitation, clearly it was no place to either leave or be left. "Ok," I quickly corrected myself, "perhaps we should leave it until we are close to a town or something. At least then we can get some food and a drink."

"Are you going to give me a hand or not?" With his glasses misting over under the strain of pulling stuff out of the boot and the frustration at seeing us standing there, it was clear Wilcox was about to blow his stack. "I'm just about bloody pissed off with this, come on get them out!"

That was it, I'd heard enough. I pulled, first mine and then Danny's rucksacks out of the boot. I tried to be as polite and unassuming as I could, "Look, thanks for the lift mate, but I think that if you feel upset then perhaps we should make our own way now and leave you to sort out the puncture."

"First, I'm not your bloody mate and second, you should be grateful for me having taken you this far," he snorted, "go on just fuck off!" He turned his back on me and began rummaging through the boot looking for his car jack and spare wheel.

We heard mutterings coming from inside the boot as we hefted the rucksacks onto our shoulders – "fucking country, fucking hitch-hikers, wish I'd never met the fucking bleeders – where's the fucking wheel-brace, I'll crack your fucking heads with it!– fucking car – oh fuck it, fuck, fuck, fuck it" Not bad for a supposedly mild-mannered, be-speckled, self-confessed wine connoisseur from Chelmsford.

It was time to move on before murder was committed!!

"C'mon Dan let's get out of here before he kills someone," I felt desperate, the man had changed into a monster and I wasn't prepared to hang around, lift or no lift. I hurried away from the car, hunched over under the weight of the rucksack, Danny just a few feet behind me.

"Whadya reckon got into him?" Danny pulled alongside of me.

"I don't know, and I don't care," I replied breathlessly. The sun was blazing down mercilessly, I was already beginning to regret our actions. But there was no going back and, what is more, this was part of our adventure. We were going to have to take the rough with the smooth. Nevertheless, I kept glancing back as Wilcox and his car slowly disappeared into the distance, just to make sure he wasn't going to race up behind us and run us off the road – the bloke had turned into a jibbering maniac all in the space of a few minutes!!

We trudged on slowly, the road was dead straight and there wasn't a sign of a car or lorry coming in either direction. I checked my watch it read close to midday and my mouth felt dry and parched. The heat was making the road shimmer and as I turned to look back along the way we had come I thought I could see a speck of movement coming towards us.

"Look out I think there's a car coming Dan," I said, feeling my spirits raise, "let's make this one count even if it just gets us out of this bloody sun."

"Ok," replied Danny and he hefted his rucksack down off his back and set it with the union jack, his mum had thoughtfully sown onto the front pocket, facing any oncoming traffic.

We stood erect, put on our happiest faces, stuck our thumbs out and muttered quiet pleadings under our breath – "come on come on, - keep smiling keep smiling, please stop, go on please." The car slowly approached – it was becoming clearer now – oh no, it was Wilcox!!

We stepped sharply back just in case, at the last minute, the idiot decided to mow us down. But no, he pulled up next to us and slowly wound his window down. "Hello lads, where are you off to?"

I tried to smile, thinking maybe we had been a bit too hasty and perhaps we should accept his offer of a lift. "Well even if you could just get us to the nearest town and drop us there, it would help." I couldn't avoid sounding like I was pleading with him.

"Hmm well, you know what, perhaps I could just do that for you, but why the fuck should I? Na you just stay there and suffer, maybe some other mug will come along eventually." He laughed almost maniacally shouting out "Tossers!" as the car lurched forward, slowly picking up speed as it disappeared into the hazy distance.

"What a bastard," bemoaned Danny, "I'm gonna have to stop for a while I feel knackered. It was obvious he had no intentions of walking another step, at least for a while and I had to admit that I felt the same way.

"Ok, yeah, you're right," I replied and pulled my rucksack away from the side of the road onto the edge of the field of vines. I positioned the rucksack against a stake supporting a vine, sat down and leaned back against it. The relief was immediate, and I was overcome with tiredness – the events of the past couple of days in the arms of Marie-France were beginning to catch up with me.

Danny parked himself down next to me, "God that feels better," he said, "lets give ourselves a few minutes to recover.

****

"Hello boys are you alright – Wakey, wakey! Are you looking for a lift?"

I tried to open my eyes and engage my brain at the same time – clearly without too much success. Danny was having a bit more luck and nudged me, none to gently, in the ribs. "C'mon mate, it's a lift!"

"Too right it's a lift but hurry up about it we haven't got all day!" came the laughing response from inside the car. I rubbed my eyes and checked my watch, it was reading three, blimey we had been there for near on two and a half hours – we could have been murdered in our beds I thought! - I struggled up. Danny was already standing next to the car, "Hi yes," I heard him say, "we're heading up towards Nantes, is that anywhere near where you're going?"

"We can certainly help you chaps on the way," came the reply, "we're heading further up the coast and, I guess, it won't take us too far out of our way to get you onto the right road at least."

Our spirits lifted instantly as our saviour jumped out of the car and walked us round to the back where he lifted the boot lid. We dropped our rucksacks thankfully into the boot and clambered into the back of the car which turned out to be a rather impressive Humber Sceptre – clearly this couple were not short of a bob or two.

"So, have you been waiting there long?" the question was asked by the doe-eyed blonde sitting in the front passenger seat, "Larry, I'm Phoebe by the way, noticed you both lying there, we thought you had been hit or something. It was only when he shouted out that we realised that you were both asleep." She gave us a warm, almost come hither, smile and I couldn't help but notice the skirt riding up her lightly tanned thighs and the blouse, open provocatively to reveal a perfect left breast – God, she wasn't even wearing a bra!

"Yeah," replied Danny, before I could jump in, "we'd been on the road for a while, we were kicked out of the last car by this bloke cos we weren't able to help him repair his puncture. We didn't have a clue what to do and to be honest I reckon he may have done for us with his wheel brace if we had stuck around too long."

"Ooh, poor you," cooed Phoebe, "you don't need to worry about that with Larry, he's a master with the wheel brace and more than capable of mending any little problems that may crop up, aren't you darling." She winked at Larry and ran her tongue around her lips. He smiled, squeezed her knee and blew a warm kiss.

I let my head fall back into the soft leather of the seat and closed my eyes as the car accelerated effortlessly away – at last we were back on our travels.

"So where have you boys been to and what have you been up to?" Phoebe had twisted round and was looking directly at me. "Not been misbehaving with the French mademoiselles I hope." She laughed and gave me a wicked look. I felt my cheeks redden under her stare. "Oh, you have, do tell!" She almost squealed, "I think we have picked up a couple of young Romeos darling!" There was an electric chemistry between Phoebe and Larry and I couldn't take my eyes off the way she reached out to touch his hand as he took the car up through the gears. I watched excitedly when she left her hand on the stick, moulding it provocatively between her fingers – blimey I was getting a hard on! "Yeah, well we've only been over here for a few days and haven't had much opportunity to meet many girls just yet." I stuttered and looked down to avoid her eyes. "Yeah right!!" laughed Danny, "I could have left him back in that crummy place we've just left. He was in pieces leaving that French floozie behind."

"Now, now please don't be too rude about the girls over here," corrected Phoebe, "so, the charm of the British male has left yet another foreign maiden feeling lost and forlorn. Mourning over whether she will ever see him again."

Larry laughed out loud and sounded the horn almost as a way of celebrating a conquest. An old couple tending the vines in the field next to the road stood up and the old boy raised his hand in a gesture of confused acknowledgement for perhaps a friend who may have passed. "I say good for you, old chap, spread the British seed far and wide, that's what I say. By the way, what's your names?"

"Steady on!" interrupted Phoebe, "any seed spreading will be carried out under strict control and only by members, and I use that word very loosely, who have been strictly vetted to ensure they are in tip top health. So be careful what you say Lawrence." She laughed and wrapped her arm round Larry's shoulder and blew a kiss into his ear.I was beginning to lose the plot.

"I'm Martin and this is Danny and it wasn't like that at all, we just met a couple of girls and they were very nice, but we didn't do anything, honest." What was I trying to do? I didn't need to make any excuse to them I could tell them anything I wanted, and they wouldn't give a damn what I said. But I was still trying to explain that I was a nice boy and not some sort of rampant bull. But Phoebe did have lovely legs and I couldn't take my eyes off them – time to sit back, shut my mouth and let my jeans loosen up a bit.

We continued for a few miles in silence and, with the gentle hum of engine and the sun streaming in through the window. I felt my eyes getting heavier and heavier. I stood in the warm shallows of the shore, the waves lapped gently around my ankles. The sun was beating down on my tanned chest as the breeze blew my tousled hair across my face, I looked up and into the distance and took a long pull on the Gauloise before flicking it nonchalantly to one side. I turned to look towards the beach and saw Marie-France jumping up and down and waving excitedly to me. "Marty, I love you!" She slipped out of her top and shorts revealing a delightful pink and blue bikini, showing her lithe figure to its best effect. She blew me a kiss, and I made to catch it in the air before returning it back towards her. "I love you too Marie-France!" She started to walk towards me and, as we met, the waves swirling around us, she smiled and slipped her arms around my neck leaning towards me, her lips aching to meet mine. I pulled her closer and felt her warmth against me revelling in the soft aroma of her perfume.
"Hey up!! Look what I see coming up ahead." I was jerked back out of my reverie by Danny's hurried exclamation, "it's that old bastard Wilcox." Danny was leaning forward between the two front seats, pointing

excitedly ahead at the be-speckled figure jumping up and down, waving his arms in front of the old car. He was clearly upset and even from a distance we couldn't help but notice the state of him, oily black smudges up to his elbows and on his previously crisp, clean shirt. The cars bonnet open and supported, precariously, by what looked to be an old length of wood. Steam was billowing out from somewhere in the engine.

"Oooh is that the fellow who threatened you with his wheel-brace?" asked Phoebe, "he doesn't look dangerous enough to me, in fact he looks rather sweet in a bookish sort of way."

Larry slowly approached the car and, as he drew level with a clearly frustrated Wilcox, wound the window down. "I say old chap, having a spot of bother?"

"I should say so," I heard the familiar whining voice, "wonder if you can give me a lift into the next town, need to get someone out to take a look at the old jalopy."

"Well, we're a bit full I'm afraid, but I'm happy for you to jump in if you don't mind squeezing into the back." Wilcox's look of gratitude was a sight to behold, and he turned back to close up the car. "That would be wonderful, I'm so grateful, I'd almost given up on anyone coming along," he called over his shoulder.

"This should be interesting," Phoebe guffawed. Danny and I looked at each other and smirked. "Better squeeze up," said Danny looks like you're in the middle." I grimaced and slid across the seat.

The bonnet lid came down with a resounding thud and Wilcox leaned down heavily on it to make sure it was properly closed. "Won't be a jiffy, don't want to leave the old girl open to any pilferers eh what. She's my pride and joy, just a little temperamental at times," he smiled at Larry and walked back over to the Humber and pulled open the rear door, "what the fu… you!!" He took a couple of steps back, seeing our smiling faces beaming out at him from the back of the Humber. "No!! I can't get in there with those two the little bastards." It was clear we had had a profound effect on Wilcox.

"Yes, yes, we've heard from these boys what happened, please keep the language civil, there's a good chap, no need for that especially with a lady present," he leaned over, winked and squeezed Phoebe's knee again, "I believe you threatened them with a wheel-brace, now are you getting in the car? I suggest you do so pretty quickly we need to be on our way." Larry was clearly not going to stand for any nonsense and so Wilcox reluctantly pushed himself into the back of the Humber and was jerked back into the seat as we accelerated away.

I could feel the heat emitting from his sweating body and the atmosphere in the car had taken a, less than pleasant, odour. The effect became over-powering and in no time all the windows had been wound down to let in some fresh, French, air.

We carried on in silence for a few miles until Phoebe turned and gave him a winning smile. "So, are you going to forgive these two young gentlemen Mr ahh, Wilcox?"

"Neville, call me Neville please. Well, I don't seem to have much choice really, I suppose." He whined, "I was just expecting a little more gratitude for having offered them a lift and yet all they wanted to do was lounge in my car without any offer of help while I tried to change a wheel."

"Yeah, and what were we meant to do? There you were shouting and screaming at your 'pride and joy'," Danny was showing his frustration, "and bellowing at us to get out of the car when we didn't have a clue as to what had happened. And then threatening us with your stupid wheel-brace."

"OK, ok that's enough," interrupted Larry, "if there's any more arguing I will put you all out of the car and you can sort out your differences well away out of our earshot, got it?"

Twenty minutes later we spotted the tower belonging to a church in the distance and then the sign that we were entering the town of 'Les Quatres Chemins'.

"The four roads," translated Phoebe, "I guess that means this is a cross-roads so perhaps you will find someone to help you here, though the place looks to be quite deserted. It must be siesta time."

She was right there didn't seem to be a soul around as we drove through the quiet streets. The white-washed walls of the old buildings were reflecting the bright sunlight into our eyes and it was difficult to make out the names of the small shops as we passed, slowly down what appeared to be the main street. Everywhere was closed and shuttered.

We turned a corner and came across a small square. A few tables were scattered around an open café and a couple of locals were sitting, enveloped within thick cigarette smoke, arms wrapped jealously around glasses of red wine. Larry drew up alongside and leaned out of the window, "Excusez messeurs y et il un garage pres d'ici?"

The response was a lethargic wave of the hand as one of the old boys pointed across to the other side of the square, "La Rue d'Eglise sur la droite la, deux minutes."

Larry called out his thanks and manoeuvred the car across the square and into the narrow street as he had been told. As we turned the corner Phoebe said, "there, look, a petrol pump, must be the garage. Looks like we've found a place which can help you out Mister Wilcox."

Wilcox needed no second bidding. He was out of the car like a long-dog. "Thank you so much for the lift I'm really grateful," he stared back at us through Larry's window, "and just watch out for those two in the back I wouldn't trust them any further than I could throw them."

"Don't worry, we won't come to any harm old chap," replied Larry, "I'm sure we'll be safe and good luck to you." He pushed the gear stick forward and drove smoothly away/ "I didn't like to say anything to the poor chap, but I spotted a sign on the garage door saying the garage is shut all day due to sickness but I'm afraid I couldn't put up with the smell of body odour any longer."

"Oh, darling that was rather beastly of you," reprimanded Phoebe, "but I bet you boys are probably relieved, aren't you?"

"You bet," I replied, "I was the one sitting next to him, he had terrible wind - smelt like a stale steak and kidney pie!" I had to smile at my own joke but only received a bored groan in response from the others.

****

"Well, here we go lads, this is as far as we can take you. We're heading west towards Brittany so you can hop out here." Larry had turned left off the road and pulled up in a layby. He jumped out of the car and opened the rear passenger door with a flourish. "Come on chop, chop we've still got quite a way to go." Before we knew what was happening, he had taken our bags out of the boot of the car and was placing them carefully on the grass verge. "Now if you just go back," he waved at the road we had just left, "and carry on along there for about a mile or so, you'll come to a main road, it's sign-posted to turn right to get to Nantes and some other place I can't quite remember where; Angers I think. That'll take you east and to wherever you're heading in that direction. Good luck, hope you get on alright and enjoy the rest of your trip." With that he jumped into the car and without a second glance back had disappeared leaving us in a cloud of dust and grit.

"Blimey that was quick," gasped Danny, "we didn't even get a chance to say cheerio to his bird."

"Phoebe," I corrected, "Come on let's go, no point hanging in this lay-by, let's get back onto the main road. We can make up our minds what we're going to do when we get to this right turning, he was on about." I checked my watch; it was four in the afternoon. I did not have a clue where we were, and I was anxious that we find a place to bed down for the night. I was feeling at a loss as to what to do so, with that, I hoisted my rucksack onto my shoulders and strode off.

The truth of the matter was that we had no real plan on where we would end up. All I knew was that despite the occasional pang of homesickness and the thought of having left Marie-France back in Fouras, I was not quite ready to head back home just yet.

After about half an hour walking in the blazing afternoon sun we reached the main junction. It was signposted right to Nantes, just twenty kilometres. Seemed like that was the best way to go, I knew it was a large town and so would probably have a campsite where we could pitch for the night, get some grub inside us and make a plan for where we should head from there.

****

I leaned heavily against the wall of the grubby bar aware of several pairs of rheumy eyes belonging to the local gentry watching my every move with un-disguised suspicion. We had left Nantes as quick as we could, Danny's flag sewn onto his rucksack had been spotted by some French oafs and they had obviously been out for trouble. We'd been fortunate to have been picked by our saviour in a dumper truck and we had left the area in a hail of wolf whistles and catcalls while we had responded with the usual V-signs and eff-off's. After that we had hitched along the length of the Loire valley, stopping at a few campsites along the way until we reached a small village near Orleans where we decided to stop off for a couple of days.

The campsite wasn't too bad, it was in the grounds of an old chateau and had a small bar onsite. It was a bit of a walk to get into the village but when we went in there was just a small shop where we managed to get baguette and cheese. I was beginning to get a taste for the French bread, much better that the rubbery stuff mum always bought from the Co-op back home.

On the second day we were there I volunteered to go in and get our stuff for the day and managed to get some change just in case it was time for me to get in touch with the old folks back home and just reassure them that we were still alive and kicking. The weather was really hot, and we sunbathed outside the tent, not feeling like doing anything in particular. When I'd had enough of Danny moaning that he was too hot and dragging himself into the shade of an old tree in the corner of the field we were camped in, I decided to make the call.

The telephone was wrapped hard against my ear as I waited for the connection to go through. Suddenly the earpiece burst into life, "Hello, this is the international operator are you happy to accept this reverse charge from a young man called Danny?" I heard my mother's muted "Yes, yes of course, put him through."

There was a brief pause and then "Hello Danny! Is that you, are you ok? There's nothing wrong is there?"

"Hi Mum, no everything's ok – just wanted to call to let you know we're all ok."

It had taken me a while to pluck up courage to ask the bloke behind the bar in 'Le Café de Paris' to use his phone. I had promised him, in my broken Franglais that he wouldn't have to pay for the call and, even as I dialled the international operator and asked for a reverse charge call to England, I could feel his hot breath behind me, waiting to snatch the phone out of my hand to make sure I wasn't telling him porkies. Once he was happy, he left me to my own devices.

"Where are you, have you lost your money, are you behaving yourselves? George it's Martin, he's calling from France!"

"How can he afford that?" I heard my ever-caring father shout down from wherever he was in the house.

"No, it's alright he's calling reverse charge from a bar." I heard mum reply.

"Bloody hell, does he think we're made of money and what does he think he's doing in a bar, he'll come back home a drunkard!"

"MUM!!" I was beginning to get annoyed, I had not called to cause an argument, I just wanted to let them both know I was ok – I was beginning to regret ever going into the bloody café. "I won't stay on the phone too long, don't worry, we're both ok, I just wanted to let you know everything's fine."

"Are you behaving yourselves over there and are you eating properly? Where-abouts are you? When do you plan on heading back? I've spoken with Danny's mum. Do you know if he's called her? If not, tell him I'll speak to her. Come on tell me where are you over there and what are you doing now? Oh, and I've also heard from

Pete and Frank, I think they have plans on coming over to France probably in the next few days."

I was having trouble taking everything in, mum was firing questions at me like a machine gun. "What did you say about Pete and Frank, where are they going to, did they say anything about wanting to meet up?" I was recalling a chat we had with them before Danny and I had left, they had mentioned about heading down towards Geneva. Talk about a turnaround! From moaning on about what Dan and I were doing as being a waste of time and now this, here they were, heading off themselves, I could not believe it!

"Well, they did say that you and Daniel (mum always had to be so bloody formal) had told them about a site in Geneva that you may head for, that's all I know."

So that was it! I recalled us talking about a site in a forest on the outskirts of the city, 'Le Bois-de-la-Batie'. But that was when we had not really decided where we would end up or, even whether we would bother to go off in that direction.

****

The car headlights blinded us as we sat on the verge of the main Paris to Lyon road. All thoughts of heading for Geneva had been dropped almost before we began talking about it. "Why d'we want to be meeting up with them two," questioned Danny, "they weren't exactly keen about going anywhere when we started talking about it and, anyhow we're getting on fine without them, let's do our own thing."

So that was it, a decision made in a matter of minutes, hence here we were miles from anywhere with no plan of our own, other than heading in a southerly direction to who knows where.

We dangled our feet over the edge of a grassy ditch, we had reluctantly accepted that it was going to be where we would sleep for the night. We had left the village near Orleans behind and agreed that south was the only way to go, at least for the time being – basically we didn't really have a clue about which direction to go in or why.

Luckily, the weather was dry although I could feel the dampness of the grass through my jeans, I shivered and turned to watch the traffic, still roaring past. It was nearly 10 in the evening, no chance of a lift now.

Or was there! how wrong I was – I stood up to try and find a drier patch of grass to make myself comfortable when the loud burping of a Maserati airhorn shot me out of my mindful meanderings as a large Citroen ground to a halt in a screech of tyres and grit. The front passenger window wound down, "All right mate, wanna lift?" You couldn't miss the nasal vibration of a Brummy accent.

I could not believe my luck and was next to the Citroen in a couple of strides, closely followed by Danny. "Do we!" I replied, almost gasping with relief, "where are you heading for?"

"Jest south mate," came the response, "hang on a sec," My Brummy friend turned to the driver and started talking, I couldn't make out what he was saying. After a couple of seconds, he turned back to me. "Me'n Andy are heading down tewards the Med, not sure if we'll make it all the way. This bloke," he jerked his thumb back towards the driver, "picked us up about ten miles back, seems he likes the company of hitchers so who'er we to argue."

"Sounds good to me," I said, "we're like you, just lookin' for the sun."

"Gerin then mate and lets get goin'," was the response. Danny and I hoisted our rucksacks and walked round to the back of the car. The driver jumped out and lifted the boot lid. "Viola M'sieur, I am Jean-Claude pleez clom-bin itiz un peu squishee."

His attempt at our fair language was something else! My mind was trying to work out what he was trying to tell me without much success, but we soon found out as we got into the back of the car. The bloke sitting there was huge and took half of the back seat leaving Danny and me almost sitting on each other's laps.

"Aw'right mate." A friendly greeting from another Brummy, "I'm Andy, so you headin' south, same as me 'n Pete."

"That's the idea," I replied, "dunno where we'll head up tho', just let the lifts take up." I was acting cool and worldly wise like an 'experienced hitcher' though the truth was I had the same dread in the back of my mind all the time that I may never see mum and dad ever again. And then, of course, there was Marie-France. That girl was always in the back of my mind – the time we had together in Fouras, and the beach – my lower heart ached, would I ever see her again?

The night passed in a hazy blur or car headlights and the heady sweet smell of Gauloises Disc Bleu coming from the front of the car. It felt like we were in heaven, a warm car, good company, and the feeling of heading somewhere – anywhere! The company of Pete and Andy and, of course Jean-Claude our chauffeur made me feel comfortable and, in a way secure. How long that would last of course depended on how far Jean-

Claude would be going; the minute he reached his destination would dictate that.

I stared out of the car window and spotted high mountains in the distance. It was just after four and the rising sun, still just below the horizon, was casting a purple glow over the looming grey peaks. "'ello, ezcoos me, eru awak?" Jean-Claude's voice alarm lifted me from my reverie while the others came to in a grumble of yawns and suppressed belches. "We err vairey cloz to Lyon, I muzz leaf zis row zoon et 'ead to ma maison et mon famille. Wair doo ewe wan me to ztop for ewen zay goobyeee?"

Andy was the first to react to Jean-Claude's question "Err dunno mate, sorry Jean-Claude, we're pretty easy, where're you headin' for?"

"Yeah, same as us," chipped in Danny before I had a chance to open my mouth, "We've got no real plans."

"Ma famille av an owz en Vaux en Beaujolais, eeet is en smoll taun naboot quinze kilometres from ear. I 'ave to geback pour mes raisins. Zoon we mus bigeen zee 'ervest."

"What does he mean 'raisins'," queried Danny.

"Grapes mate, grapes," said Pete, "what d'you reckon Andy, shall we do some picking, pick up a few bob?"

"Sounds like a plan to me mate, what about you two lads, fancy earning a bit of cash?"

"If he'll have us then we're up for it," I replied before Danny could butt in. I knew he wasn't a fan of work of any kind, but I also knew that my money situation could do with a bit of a leg up and if mine did then so did his. Pete turned to Jean-Claude and in near-perfect French (well it sounded perfect to me) started rattling off his idea.

"Oui oui, bien sur, nous avons beaucoup de raisins le travail est tres dur mais je vais te donner un endroit pour dormir et manger et payer aussi." Jean-Claude bounced up and down in his seat, he seemed almost ecstatic! I began to think he wasn't telling us something, I guess we'd find out fairly soon if he'd stitched us up or not, but I was all for giving it a go.

"Seems like we've got a deal," said Pete, "food, somewhere to kip and a bit of cash thrown in for good measure! Sounds like it might be hard graft, but we just stay around as long as it suits."

Thanks to Pete and his command of the French language, a hell of a lot better than listening to Jean-Claude struggling with English!

****

Vaux en Beaujolais

I'd never been up close to mountains before or driven along roads so narrow and winding. Now I was suffering from being driven at breakneck speed and with a mad Frenchman smiling and letting rip with Le Marseillaise - clearly the bloke was happy to be home. "You like my 'ome n'est ce pas?" he chirped, flinging the car round a hairpin bend, almost on two wheels. I looked out from the car window and immediately wished I hadn't bothered – there was nothing below me just a gaping emptiness and across the steep valley loomed a high mountain bathed in early morning sun. Jean-Claude flung the heavy vehicle round yet another bend and the mountain disappeared from my view. The road descended steeply into a valley and as it flattened out and the valley widened, I could see nothing but rows and rows of small vines growing on the valley sides. "There you go lads," said Pete, "we're in wine country, welcome to where you're going to start making some money."
"So, this is it," I grumbled, "hard work for the next few days, how are we going to manage it?"
"Don't worry about," replied Pete, "it won't be as bad as you think and with free food and bed thrown in who's

complaining? We did it last year for a month or two and we made enough to keeps us going for an extra couple of months over here."

"Yeah, but we don't have that long," said Danny, "need to get back at some point to get our exam results."

I suddenly woke up to the fact that our futures would be waiting for us when we finally got home, and I felt a sick feeling overcome the pit of my stomach. Would I be going back to do my A-levels or be looking for a job somewhere? "Thanks mate, I'd forgotten all about that. Think I'd like to leave it like that just for the time being." I watched the high fields drift by and then in the distance I spotted a cluster of low buildings and could also see quite a few people wandering around in the fields. So, this is where we're heading, I thought. We zig-zagged along a dusty drive for a few minutes, finally rounding a bend and there in front of us was a low barn bathed in early morning sun. I spotted an old man sitting on an up-turned barrel and leaning back against the wall.

The big car drew up sharply in a cloud of dust and Jean-Claude had his door opened and jumped out almost as soon as he had pulled on the handbrake. "Papa!" I heard hm cry out.

"Jean-Claude!" came the equally joyous response and the old boy sprang, a little unsteadily, to his feet and almost sprinted across the small yard, the off-brown cigarette which had been sticking out of his mouth was unceremoniously thrown to the ground as he wrapped Jean-Claude in a bear-like embrace while the rest of us clambered out of the car and stood around wondering what to do next.

The old boy suddenly stood back, realising that Jean-Claude had not arrived alone. He looked at us suspiciously before nodding to Jean-Claude in our direction.

"Oh pardon!" Jean-Claude suddenly remembered we were there, "c'est mon papa," and invited us forward to shake hands with his father.

Before we could dodge his advances, his unshaven face greeted us with kisses on both cheeks. He then quickly turned back to Jean-Claude engaging him on a question-and-answer session about where we'd met and what we were doing here until it dawned on him that we were the extra hands for the grape harvest.

"Ahh bon, bon welcome to my 'ouse, m'appelle Francois" he beamed, "you 'ave a bon time 'ere, plenty work et bon food. Et le vin c'est tres bon, et les filles ici, ils sont tres belle!" He winked knowingly and punched Danny, none too gently, on his shoulder.

Dan staggered back a couple of steps and blushed "Filles eh, I guess he means girls. Should be fun." He gave me a worried look which said it all – what had we let ourselves in for?

Jean-Claude sidled round to the back of the big Citroen, clicked open the bootlid and took out our rucksacks. "'ear ewe err, ewe cum wiz mee end I will tek ewe to ur bounk 'ouse wair ewe ken mek ur ome." We gratefully hoisted our rucksacks and trudged along behind him. The 'bunkhouse' looked like an old barn and not in too good repair but, as he opened the door and stood aside with an exaggerated bow, I was impressed. A large room with a dozen or so beds, all in a line and neatly made up, stood in front of us. Light streamed in from windows set high into the roof. Doors at one end, labelled 'Dames' and 'Hommes', needed no explanation.

"'Ear ewe ken sleep en wosh ouup," said Jean-Claude, "pour l'alimentation ewe ken cum eeinto our 'ouse en eat wiv uz."

"Sounds great," exclaimed Pete, "are we the only ones or will there be more coming?"

"Zer will be mooor, 'ow ewe say – skoolars? Zey cum in phew daiies wen thair 'olidays begin."

"Ah students," corrected Pete, "should be an interesting mix, I think we'll look forward to meeting them."

"Looks like it'll be an interesting mixed bag all in here together." Muttered Dan. I got the feeling he was quietly looking forward to meeting our future roommates.

John-Claude bade us farewell saying that he would come back in a short while after we had had a chance to settle ourselves in. I took myself through the door marked 'Hommes', expecting to see the dreaded 'hole leading to nowhere', but was pleasantly surprised to find that the twentieth century had reached this far-flung outback of France. I christened the porcelain bowl and returned to the 'dorm', because that was what it was, and claimed a bed as the other three had already done. Having taken off my plimsolls I lay back on the bed and closed my eyes.

"C'mon Marty wake up!!" I was shaken non-too gently by Andy who sat back down on the bed next to me, "you were out for the count mate, you must've been knackered. Anyway, we've been told to get ready to take a tour round the place and we're also keen to find out how far the local town is from here. I think Jean-Claude's mum is going to rustle up some grub."

I dragged myself into an upright position trying to figure out gather my thoughts – I felt like crap. "What's the time?"

"Just after twelve, you been out for around four hours," replied Andy, "anyhow let's get moving, can't hang around here all day."

The sun was blazing down and I could feel the weight of the heat on my shoulders as we headed out of the bunk house and walked across the yard to where Danny and Pete were waiting, Danny grunted something I couldn't make out other than "lazy bastard – 'bout time you got up" and we headed off in the direction of an old house set separately away from the other buildings and where Jean-Claude was patiently waiting. "Bonjour mes amies, pleez cum en an' meet ma maman."

We filed in through the door and were instantly cooled by the welcoming interior. Standing behind a large, scrubbed, table which was set with piles of baguettes and cheese, was a small smiling woman who quickly came around and took us, each in turn, in a fierce bear hug. She started chattering away at nineteen to the dozen to which we all responded with unknowing smiles – we couldn't understand a word!

"Pleeez zit mi frenzz," said Jean-Claude, "ma maman, duz nozpeek zee aingleesh well lik moi, mais elle zays weelcum an wanzz ewe to manger."

We all obeyed and, within seconds, were presented with a pitcher of red wine which Jean-Claude poured generously into the glass tumblers sitting alongside the food. He raised his glass, "Salut, mi frenzz I 'op ewe enjoy yuur tim whyl ewe errr wiv uzz." I was having trouble stopping myself from bursting into laughter – the more I heard him the funnier it was getting.

The food was delicious, I didn't realise how hungry I was, but then it had been a long time since Dan and I had last eaten. Jean-Claude explained the workings of the vineyard and what we were expected to do. From what we could make out, he was expecting a few others, mainly students, to arrive in the next couple of days and said that we wouldn't be expected to start until they had arrived. We also found out that the nearest village, Vaux-en-Beaujolais, was only a couple of kilometres away. We quickly decided that we should explore it that evening.

Having taken it easy for the remainder of the afternoon we all felt refreshed, particularly after Madam's meal and made an effort to smarten ourselves up for our reconnoitre of local village life.

Jean-Claude came over to the bunkhouse to wish us well on our first trip out. "I 'ave zis lyet vor ewe. Pliz tak eat, ze rod indoo ze villaage est ver darg end ve don ave menee voitures ear mais eat vill keeep ewe save". We made our goodbyes and headed off, in the last of the afternoon heat, towards Vaux we were in good spirits.

The village of Vaux-en-Beaujolais was more of a small town than a village with plenty of small shops and bars, certainly bigger than we had expected. Some of the stores were closed, but it was good to see that a few of them were beginning to open after their prolonged afternoon siesta.

We found ourselves in a small square which was busy with a few small market stalls, many of which were being dismantled – obviously we had missed their weekly market. But a couple were still going strong, trying to get rid of the last of their wares, mainly fruit and veg.

We made our way towards the din coming from a small bar further along the street. A symphony of shrieks and chatter hit us as we reached the door. "This is more like it", grinned Danny, "c'mon in we go". A few of the locals turned round and stared as we entered but quickly turned back to their drinks, clearly reassured that we posed no threat to the enjoyment of their evening. I went straight to the bar catching the eye of the owner who was quietly talking to a local at the other end of the bar, he smiled and sauntered up to me. "Oui m'sieur?" " "Bonjour, quatre bieres presion, s'il vous plait." I was beginning to gain confidence in my French and knew that showing them that I wasn't afraid to practice the language would earn their respect. Our beers quickly arrived, and we looked around.

From the dark bowels of the bar the stereophonic voice of Ray Davis and the Kinks was gainfully belting out "You really got me" above the din. A small group of kids were standing around the old jukebox their heads nodding up and down as though worshipping at an electronic altar. The occasional "Yeah groovy man this is the real thing – Got me Going yeaaahh n'est ce pas" as they jigged and jogged to the number one in the French charts – always a few years behind the English I observed quietly to myself.

Our first evening venture into Vaux eventually came to a pleasant ending and, having managed to down a few glasses of the local bieres, plus a few proffered cigarettes from, what turned out to be, the friendly locals we eventually made our au revoirs to the village. The fresh air hit me with a vengeance and, through the haze rapidly engulfing my brain I realised that the beer I considered no better than cat-pee had a far stronger effect. The walk back was broken up by several stops to relieve ourselves, and despite my inebriated state, I realised that my aim was somewhat uncertain, managing to hit not only the tree but also the back of Dannys' jeans. It took us more than an hour weaving along the dark lane back to what would be our home for the next however many days or weeks. But we made it and hitting the pillow on my bed was my last recollection of the day.

Cerraaash!! My fuddled brain was hit by a noise not unlike a jet going through the sound barrier – not that I'd ever heard a jet going through the sound barrier!

Dannngggg!! There it was again and, despite the state of my head and the sledge hammer trying to bash a hole through my brain, I shot up out of my bed.

"Wha's going on," I heard myself yell out. I wasn't alone, the other three in our 'dormitory' were also gazing dazedly around wondering what the hell was happening.

"Bonjour mes amis!! Velcum tu un beau jour end un eyek fruu ur lurrvry feelds de vin." Jean-Claude stood at the foot of our beds holding a large dinner gong which he repeatedly clouted with his fist.

"Ok, ok enough already," grumbled Pete, "we heard you – we're coming ok."

"C'est un belle jour meye frens, c'est teyem tu injoy ur lurrvry countree. Ma maman avez les croissants et café weigh-ting fer-u. Cum don let eat ger gold." Clearly, he was enjoying himself although, to be fair, he seemed to have a permanent smile on his face – obviously a happy Frenchman, content with his life.

We dragged ourselves out of bed and, stretching into upright positions, reluctantly followed our tormentor out of the bunkhouse. I immediately noticed that it was barely light, I could just see the rim of the sun as it cast a pale glow across the far hills. The sky was clear with not a cloud in the sky, and I figured that it promised to be a warm day ahead, but what a bloody awful time to be dragged out of bed. For the first time I checked my watch – 6 o'clock for god's sake!!

We filed through the door of the large farmhouse kitchen and were hit by the warm aroma of coffee and fresh baked bread – I could feel my spirits, as well as the pain in my head lifting. Jean-Claudes mother was standing by the old range and smilingly beckoned us to sit down around the table with Jean-Claude at the head. As we settled down the door at the far end of the kitchen opened and his father entered. Jean-Claude immediately stood and moved around to the side of the table, he gave his father a deferential nod and the old man smiled back in return.

"Bonjour," said his father and sat down magisterially, leaning forward as he did so to take a long baguette, which he broke into several smaller pieces, placing them back onto the table. "Pleez take somet'ing to eat," he pointed to the bread and the selection of meats and cheeses which his wife had also placed down on the table. "Eat well my frens we 'ave a busy day today."

I needed no second bidding and grabbed a couple of lumps of bread and a selection of meats – I was starving. Madam poured us all a coffee and as I took my first swig the last of the hammering in my head disappeared into oblivion, to be replaced by a hit of strong, black coffee that made my toes curl, certainly a great cure for a hangover.

While we may have entered the kitchen in a stony silence, we left a lot cheerier, even Danny appeared to be in a good mood – he was never one for early mornings, I always remembered my mum telling me what his mum had said about his getting up particularly on school days – it wasn't good listening!

Jean-Claude led us across the yard and along a narrow lane, wide enough for a tractor I guessed. We carried along for around fifteen minutes before arriving at the edge of a large field full of rows and rows of low straggly bushed, probably no more than six feet high. They were kept in place by thin wire fences which ran along each row. The bushes were in full leaf and I could see that each carried several bunches of red grapes.

"Theez is vwat ve ave cum topick, pleeez treye zum," said Jean-Claude. I wasted no time, I loved grapes, and I stepped forward to the nearest bush and tore out two or three of the largest grapes. I was immediately taken back by the sharp taste even though much juicier that the ones mum bought from Fine Fare.

"C'est bon n'est pas?" said Jean-Claude, "Zis vil be ur fist ervest of zis yer en vill be ze erly Beaujolais, redee en Novembre. Il s'apple le Beaujolais Nouveau. Demaine ve vill star peeking ven udders vill be errreyevin to elp. Mais pour aujourd-hui I vill showe ewe vat ewe ave to do ok?"

Jean-Claude stretched his back, twisting to and fro to ease his muscles from where he had been bending

over the vines. "OK, I zink ewe ave ad eeenuff teyem wiv me, maintenant nous allons retourner a la ferme end ewe ken 'ave zee res of zee day a vous memes."
I, for one, was grateful, we had been in the field for not much more than a couple of hours, wandering up and down the rows of vines while he showed us which bunches of grapes we should pick and which we should avoid. It was bloody had work, bent over all the time and my back was feeling pretty sore. I was also struggling to make sense of what he was saying!!
The sun had also risen high into the sky and was burning a hole into my neck – I'd have to find a hat from somewhere otherwise I'd end up in agony. Danny, Pete and Andy looked like they all three felt the same and we were grateful to get back to the bunkhouse for a rest.
"Don't call this much of a bloody holiday," mumbled Danny as we lay on our beds, trying to catch our breath after the walk back from the fields, "don't think we'll be spending too long in this place, what d'you reckon?"
"Think you might be right," I murmured, "but let's give it a few days, he's paying us at the end of each week, and I could do with a bit of a top up of funds, plus we're being fed which also helps." The truth was my money pot had run dangerously low mainly due to spending

too much on drink in Fouras. I had been tempted to dip into my return fare back to Blighty but I knew that, if that happened, I'd be in real trouble.

"OK let's give it a week then," said Danny, "how about you two?" he looked round at Pete and Andy.

"We'll probably hang around here for a couple of weeks or so," replied Pete, "we're in no hurry to get back, our results are not due for a few weeks yet".

There it was again, the reminder that we had to go back to getting our O-level results! I could feel a wave of depression wash over me as my mind took me back to the reality of life. "Don't talk about exam results I moaned," burying my head in the pillow "that's the last thing I want to think about while I'm over here."

"Don't start moaning about that, tell you what, why don't we head back into the village later," suggested Danny, "I think I saw a poster saying that there was something going on in their village hall this evening, it might be fun and must be better than hanging around here." Andy and Pete agreed and, while I wasn't bothered either way, I agreed to tag along.

The village hall, as Danny had called it had clearly seen better days but, as we went through into the bright interior a big effort had been made to welcome tonight's audience for what we hoped would be a fun packed evening.

An elderly woman was sitting at a table just inside the main entrance, "Bon soir messieurs, vous avez un billet?" she asked though a cloud of smoke coming from the Gauloise clamped firmly between her teeth. Clearly, we hadn't expected to have to pay.

Danny being caught off-guard quickly fell into his faltering French, "eeerrr non we don't, avez vous got any tickets we could acheter?"

"Ahh vous etes Anglais, mais oui I will sell you verrrrr good seats," she was obviously anxious to get some customers coming through the door, "dix francs pour tous."

"Ten francs for the four of us, that ain't bad," exclaimed Pete, "here you go Dan, take this, my treat, you boys can buy the drinks later." He handed Danny a ten franc note and we were soon in possession of our tickets.

"Tu peu t'asseoir n'import ou," called out the woman as we headed towards the hall.

"She says that we can sit anywhere," said Pete as we were greeted by a roar of voices and saw before us what must have been the whole elderly population of the village busy catching up with their neighbours with the local gossip – had we made a mistake coming?

It was obvious that this evening was scheduled to be a great event, so we didn't expect to be ushered by the obliging locals to seats right in front of a low stage, barely six feet from where we were expected to sit. I couldn't understand how we managed to get such good seats, my experience, gained from the Essoldo cinema back home, was that front row seats were like gold dust, what did these locals know that we didn't? – we were soon to find out.

We made ourselves comfortable on the hard canvas chairs, this would be fun I thought to myself. I turned round to get an idea of our fellow audience members, an old gent caught my eye and gave me a nod and smiled slyly, I smiled back nervously.

Ten minutes passed and then suddenly the lights were switched off around the hall leaving on only those lights immediately over the stage area and the front row of seats, our row.

I felt very exposed. An elderly gent, in what passed for an equally elderly dinner suit, wandered onto the stage to a round of muted applause, he waved sheet of paper he was holding, and the applause slowly died away. He prattled on reading from the paper giving what I assumed was to be the list of events for the evening and, having finished his speech turned around and quickly left the stage. I couldn't help but notice that the backside of his trousers hung down limply to just about his knees – he had clearly not bought that suit from John Collier!

The lights above us went off and we were left in a dark silence save for some mutterings a rasping cough and what sounded like chair legs scraping coming from directly in front of us. Suddenly the lights came back on blinding the audience for a few brief seconds and then, there he was a wrinkled old boy peering myopically over a huge accordian. We were faced with the sight of his legs, spread wide together with his grubby trousers hanging limply around his crotch area as he attempted to balance the wavering instrument on his thin bony knees.

The audience clapped politely as we all waited while he made himself comfortable, taking time to stub out the standard French item of choice, his Gauloise, under his boot. With a final hurrumph and a twitch he stretched the bellows of the instrument as wide as they would go and launched into a series of exercises, in out, in out with the machine while his right hand danced, playing up and down the keyboard. I was mesmerised, his playing was so impressive, and I watched as he seemed to be playing while in an almost trance-like state, his eyes closed as his head rocked gently from side to side. He played several pieces of music after each one taking a furtive bow while the audience, including the four of us, showed our appreciation. Finally, he came to his last number 'Le Marseilleise' and the whole audience, again including the four of us, stood to attention until the last note when he received a round of rapturous applause. I noted several coins being thrown onto the stage and was impressed by the rapidity with which he managed to untangle himself from his instrument before scrabbling around to pick up the donations. He certainly knew how to work his audience.

The next hour passed while several acts came and went to various levels of appreciation. We were treated to an elderly woman and her five performing poodles, we saw high kicks, walking on front legs only while back legs jiggled up and down while releasing a crescendo of popping farts. A farting French poodle, now I'd seen and heard everything.

Later came a small girl balancing what looked like a garden rake on her head – things went well until she lost her footing, and the rake came down in a graceful arc landing on the top of her nose – she left the stage in floods of wailing tears and a bloody nose.

At last, after the stage had been cleared of blood and other mess created by the earlier acts the compere came out to announce the final act, the star of the show! It was obvious that the audience knew what we were in for and gave vent to a number of cheers with a few cat-calls mixed in for good measure.

Again, the lights went off and we waited breathlessly while things were readied on the stage. And then, in a sudden burst on they came.

The woman was huge, a massive acknowledgement to a Rubenesque character, but with the hostile intention of swiping anyone in her way with one of her enormous breasts. She stood directly in front of where I was sitting, I was an easy target. She held both her hands across her ample belly and took in a deep breath - I felt my own need to take in more oxygen getting desperate, everything about this woman was huge, including her lung capacity. Her mouth opened and I spied the battered railings of tobacco-stained teeth ready to devour anything that came within their range! "Non reeeeeaaaaaaaan duuurrrr reeeeaaan, Non, je ne regrette reeeeaaaan." The noise was a mixture of screeches and grunts interspersed with great gulps of air to re-inflate her enormous bosom. The distance between her top and bottom set of teeth grew greater and greater and her head sprang back revealing huge nostrils the green sticky contents of which glowed from the two footlights thoughtfully positioned on the makeshift stage - I hoped it would remain in place for the duration of the performance. I watched too, fascinated, as great globs of grey spittle stretched, almost delicately, between her top and bottom lips where they occasionally broke and sprang back as she continued to ruin the Edith Piaff classic. I quietly prayed that the same thing didn't happen to one of her bra straps, God only knows what would happen if one of those huge appendages were let loose – and I was in the direct firing line!!

The final straw came as she reached the end of the final verse, "Ca commence aaaavec toi!!", and began, for some inexplicable reason, to prance around the makeshift stage. The boards creaked under the pressure of her huge feet as they tip-toed around in ever decreasing circles, her arms flailing up and down trying to depict some giant bird attempting, without success, to head skywards – clearly the runway was too short!

She came to a sudden halt, clearly out of breath but never prepared to accept that she was physically incapable of what was to be her magnificent finale. She stood stock still and I watched as she leant forward on her left leg whilst raising her right leg behind her – it reminded me of a dog having a pee against a lampost. Was this the end of her performance?

Without thinking I leapt to my feet to applaud her valiant effort, secretly hoping that it would be enough encouragement for her to leave the stage.

The hall remained silent as I stood there feeling suddenly exposed and alone. Danny, sniggeringly, grabbed me by the arm attempting to pull me down onto my seat. On the stage the woman stood there, staring at me, her face glazed over in an almost terrified rictus. She remained frozen in her compromised position for what seemed an eternity until she finally gave way, slowly at first, while she tried to regain her balance before crashing unceremoniously onto the stage.

A terrified silence preceded the sudden roar as the audience behind us came to their senses and I felt myself being pushed and shoved aside by several elderly men as they fell over themselves to get to the stricken woman. What followed was much grunting and groaning as they struggled to get her into a sitting position.

I noticed that they made full use of the situation to ensure their hands assisted every part of her massive body – she did not seem to be unduly concerned at this intimate intrusion. As they raised her up, I could see that she was covered in a fine, white coating of dust which I quickly realised was the result of ash falling from several Gitanes and Gauloises which continued to cling to the lips of her gallant rescuers.

I remained sitting in my seat, my eyes transfixed on the events taking place before me. Eventually I ventured to turn round and was met by the accusing stares from several elderly women sitting several rows behind me – I couldn't help but notice that they were all sitting next to empty chairs and realised that they must be the wives of the old boys who had dashed onto the stage to rescue the stricken diva.

"Well done," laughed Andy, in an effort to make himself heard above the din, "you've certainly brought the evening to a great conclusion". I smiled uncertainly and couldn't help noticing the smirk spread across his face. At last, the chaos was being brought under control and several of the rescuers were heading back to their seats, clearly worried as to what wrath they may face from their other halves. However, I was buoyed up by the satisfied grins on some of their faces and even felt quite elated when one old boy gave me a friendly slap on the shoulder while quietly whispering in my ear, "Merci, bon chance eh" as he headed back to an uncertain future.

It was clearly time for us to make our departure and we left the hall to the sound of raised, indignant, female voices behind us.

Out in the cool evening air I was able to regain some of my own composure and realised that I would be able to feast on this story when we eventually arrived back home in blighty. I might even be able to make a bit out of it in the way of free smokes and even the occasional drink – clearly a job well done!

We headed back to the bar we had found the previous day, reflecting on the evenings' entertainment, agreeing that we had enjoyed rural France at its' very best – wasn't that why we had come over for in any case, to sample Gallic life in its' rawest form?

The bar was still open and music was again blaring out of the jukebox. We bustled through the half-dozen or so locals and gathered around a table next to the bar. "My round", I said, forgetting that my funds were a little low, "I think I deserve it after that."

Beers were ordered and we sat while they were pulled and then delivered by the bar owners' doe-eyed daughter Madelaine. She sidled across to our table humming some sort of seductive French ditty and pushed up against Danny as the four glasses were placed on the table. She gave him a smile that shouted out one of two possible messages, either 'I think you're quite cute and would like you to ask me out for the evening' or 'you look like a bit of a smart-arse and I'm going to embarrass you in front of your mates'. His face turned puce, and I took the opportunity to nudge him in the ribs, "Hey mate she fancies you, go on now's your big chance get in there Danny boy!"

"Fuck off," came the retort, "not my type." As he took a swig of his cold beer. The three of us fell about laughing at his obvious embarrassment. How would life work out for Danny the intrepid Lothario?

The following day again dawned early, but this time we were ready for it, having only had a couple of drinks before leaving the bar. We had to make a good impression on Jean-Claude – nice as he was, I reckoned he could be a bit of a taskmaster.

Sure enough, the dinner gong sounded ahead of the sun appearing on the horizon and we dragged ourselves out of the bunkhouse and into madam's kitchen. There we were welcomed by the warm aroma of fresh coffee and freshly baked bread.

"Are you ready for picking our beautiful raisins aujourd'hui?" came the cheerful question from Jean Claude's father as he dipped his croissant into a bowl of steaming hot chocolate.

"Like a hole in the head," mumbled Danny as he dragged his chair across the flagstone floor, "could do with a few more hours kip to be honest." Pete, Andy and I couldn't help noticing the sarcastic emphasis Dan had placed on the aitch in honest – he was clearly getting fed up with having to endure the use of broken English.

"C'mon mate," chipped in Andy, "you'll be paid in a few days and then, with a few francs rattling around in your pocket you can treat the lovely Madelaine to a first date." We roared laughing and I couldn't help but notice that despite his grimace, Dan had a slight glimmer in his eye.

Having had our fill of Madam's delicious breakfast we set off to the vine fields and we were soon armed with baskets and clippers ready to attack the fruits. I was quietly relieved that we started early as, with my back arched over the vines it was not easy work. As the sun rose slowly over the distant hills the temperature began to soar and I could feel myself begin to feel it on my back. Jean-Claude, ever attentive to our needs, gave us all large, wide-brimmed, hats and bottles of water for which I was soon grateful as this was not my idea of fun.

After around four hours of toil, he called a halt "Ok mes amis, I zink ewe av ad inufff fer un vile. Ve vill 'ave un vest und zooon zey vill cum viv zum vood und trink." We gratefully dropped down our tools of the trade and headed over to a small hut in the corner of the field. No sooner had we settled down on the hard chairs, I spotted two long-legged beauties heading towards us pulling a small handcart. I immediately tore off my hat and ran my fingers through my hair, I couldn't be seen looking like some common labourer in front of such magnificent creatures.

"Ahhh bon ze rilif is et and!" shouted Jean-Claude and he jumped up and strode purposefully across to where they were pulling the cart up the final slope. They could give me some relief anytime they wanted, I thought to myself. Jean-Claude took both girls in his arms and hugged them close – obviously these were not strangers: at least not to him. The four of us stood up as one and I couldn't help but notice that they had had the same idea as me – hats off in an attempt to smarten up and make a good impression.

"Plizz met mes deux soeurs, Giselle et Claudine. Zey 'ave cum frerm zeir stoodies a zerr uni verzeetea de Lyons und er ear to elp uz."

The girls were stunning, if they were dressed for working then I was all for it. Tight jeans turned up above the ankles and virgin white blouses barely covering sumptuous bodies, I was smitten. Both kissed by the sun their dark, come hither eyes focussed on each of us in turn and I could feel my toes curling in embarrassment as they seemed to be grading us on suitability as a mate.

Giselle, the taller of the two (by no more than an inch) pushed her hair back from her face and fluttered her eyes at Danny who stood there with his mouth slightly open, looking like a gargoyle, frozen in time. I could tell at once that she was a definite prick-teaser and was leading him up the garden path. "Bonjour mes amis," she breathed, keeping her eyes fixed on my poor stricken friend, "I 'ope you err aving fun werking wis my brozzer. What err your nams?" – at least I could understand her better than Jean-Claude --. Danny, giving a great impression of a goldfish out of water blurted out his name and turned a deep shade of puce. He was closely followed by the rest of us.

We were all then treated to the standard French welcome of a kiss on each cheek, but I couldn't help but notice that, after our initial introduction they were paying more attention to Pete and Andy than Dan and me. Clearly, we were the babes of this group and probably out of their league.

Jean-Claude took his sisters to one side and they prattled on for several minutes before he remembered why they were there. He pulled back a cloth from the handcart to reveal a plate loaded with baguettes and a pitcher of what looked suspiciously like wine – drinking on the job, could be a toxic mix!

****

I stood, unable to move, as the blazing lights came closer and closer, the screeching noise bore into my head forcing me to close my eyes tighter. Where was I, what was happening to me?? My head was pounding and then I looked up. I was standing in the path of a roaring monster. It was a train heading straight for me! The screeching of the monsters' wheels and the scream of its' horn bore into me shaking me to the core. I couldn't move, I was transfixed, almost in a state of trance. I tried to open my eyes to see better what was going on around me. And then it hit me full in the head and I reeled over groaning as reality struck. My eyes were watering; the explosion when it came ground me further into my pillow and I wrapped the covers around me to keep everything away, I just wanted to die.

A few short seconds later realisation struck – I was well and truly hungover! The previous day was a blur - I could remember heading to the vines in the morning and the arrival of Jean-Claude with his two gorgeous sisters bringing food – and the wine!! Ah yes, the wine – we had sat ourselves down in the shade, the girls had spread a large, chequered cloth over the ground and prepared the feast. We had taken turns at swigging the deep red liquid from the pitcher, it had been bottomless coming round and round between each of us and taking yet one more swig. I had pretty much ignored the baguettes, determined to get my fill of the liquid gold – would I ever learn?

How did I get back to the bunkhouse? I didn't have a clue – I was still fully dressed apart from my plimsols. My head was banging, every time I tried to lift it from my pillow it became even worse. I was certain my brain had shrunk and was slapping against the sides of my head. I tried to open my mouth it was so dry, my tongue felt like it had swollen to twice its size and seemed stuck, unable to move.

I felt something sweet and moist around the edges of my lips. I strained to open my eyes and there, through the haze, sitting on my bed was Madame, Jean-Claudes' mum. She was saying something to me, I couldn't make out what. Her hand had worked its' way round the back of my head and was gently trying to lift me off the pillow while, with her other hand, she held a glass of water to my dry and parched lips, I had never tasted anything so good.

A sudden wave of embarrassment hit me as I realised, with each passing second, where I was and what I must look like. I tried to sit myself up but was held firmly back as Madame pushed the small glass into my hand with a firm "l'eau, buvez." I took a few faltering sips and, almost without thinking poured the remaining contents into my grateful mouth.

I suddenly realised Madame was not alone for there, standing behind her, was Monsieur a broad smile spread across his face. "Vous avez goute le nectar du Beaujolais, c'est bon eh?" With that he turned and walked out quietly chuckling to himself.

I looked around me, nobody else was around, no Danny, Pete, or Andy. "Where are my mates?" I stammered, "mes amis?"

Madame look at me and smiled, "Tes amis? Ils sont chez mois en train le diner."

Dinner! I suddenly realised I was starving, my belly felt like my throat had been cut!! I attempted to sit up but the pounding in my head put an abrupt end to that. I dug my fists hard into my eyes and felt my hand pulled away as another glass of water was pushed into it. I drank greedily. Madame took the empty glass away from me and stood up, she looked down at me and with hands firmly placed on her hips said, "you stand!" I couldn't argue against that order so swung my legs gingerly round onto the side of the bed and with a quiet "one two," pushed myself up to where she was waiting to steady me.

With the help of Madam I staggered out and made my way cautiously across the yard into the house. A great cheer rose as I walked through the door. There were the others gathered around the large kitchen table, a pile of bread and cheeses balanced precariously in the middle.

"Welcome back to the land of the living!" quipped Andy and the others joined in with their own personal greetings. Despite my condition I couldn't help but notice that Giselle and Claudine were there and had miraculously matched themselves with Pete and Andy – I felt a pang of jealousy as I dropped into the empty chair next to Danny and leant my elbows on the table, head in my hands.

"Never again I muttered, I feel bloody awful". And it was no exaggeration my head was roaring, and my belly was doing somersaults, I had never felt so bad in my life!

"Fancy a beer?" laughed Danny, "or how about a nice greasy bacon sarnie?" I quietly muttered a dismal "eff off" in reply and remained wallowing in my own personal hell.

"Best thing for you is some bread and maybe a bit of cheese," recommended Pete, "you need to get something inside you, it'll make to feel a whole lot better." I took him at his word and tore off a small hunk of bread – it was like manna from heaven!! The effect was almost instantaneous, I followed it with heavy gulps of water from the cup Danny pushed towards me. "God that's better," I mumbled, "that's the last time I ever drink that much." The truth was I couldn't remember how much wine I had swallowed – I couldn't remember anything about the afternoon at all, including how I made it back to the bunkhouse. But very slowly I was beginning to regain my senses, the cocktail of bread and water was working its' magic.

"Don't worry mate, we've all been there," grinned Andy, "and it won't be the last time for you either. In fact, hair of the dog may be in order."

"What!" I shouted as hard as my aching throat could muster, "you must be kiddin', I'm telling you, if I had one more drop of that bloody wine, I'd throw my guts up!"

"No Andy's right," said Pete, "a cold beer or two would help get rid of the taste of the wine and may also clear your head. Think about it, you've had a bit to eat, and the best thing now is to stay up so when you do go to bed it'll be because you're tired, not pissed."

And so it was that an hour or so later I found myself trudging along the narrow lanes heading for Vaux. Our number had swelled to six, with Giselle and Claudine walking arm in arm with Andy and Pete respectively. Danny and I were a few yards in front. Buoyed by Madame's delicious bread and cheese and, of course cupsful of clear, cold water I was actually feeling much better.

Not too sure whether I was looking forward to my first sip of beer, but I was glad that I hadn't remained back in the bunkhouse feeling sorry for myself.

"You could have scored there," I whispered to Danny as I took a sly peep behind me, just in time to see Giselle's tongue furtively licking around Andy's ear – my god that girl wasn't wasting any time that was a fact, - "she was yours for the taking." I winked.

He looked at me with the worse hang-dog expression I had ever seen. "You must be joking, I wasn't in her league and you know it. Just like that bird you met in Fouras she was too classy for you by a mile."

I made to punch him on the arm. "That was different, she gave up that drongo Brad so she could be with me. She really liked me, wish we'd stayed around a bit longer. Anyway, that was your fault you wanted to leave with that prick Wilcox." I could feel my temper rising, I wanted to defend what happened between me and Marie-France. "anyway, you fucked up with her mate Nicole, otherwise things could have gone different and we could both be happy how things turned out."

"Ok, ok, I'm sorry," replied Danny, "but as for Giselle she's with Andy and that's that, you win some, you lose some. Come on let's forget about it and get to that bar."

We quickened our pace but, when I turned round, I could see that Pete, Andy and the girls were slowing down. I nudged Danny, "They'll be heading into the bushes in a few minutes," I quipped, "come on let's not waste any more time waiting for them to catch up."

We carried on into the village and headed into the bar, which was beginning to become our 'local' – not bad for a couple of sixteen-year-olds who would have been kicked out of the pub if we had tried it back in good old England!! Surprisingly we were joined a few minutes later by the others – clearly they hadn't managed to find any suitable bushes!

We ordered our beers at the bar and found a table next to the juke box which was pumping out some obscure French rock number which, when I asked to few kids who were hanging around the box, turned out to be the latest Johnny Hallyday number – we were unimpressed. "Don't worry," I whispered to the others, "I know what these guys like," and walked over with a couple of francs to punch in some of the Kinks and Rolling Stones. It was an instant success.

The beers arrived courtesy of the lovely Madelaine who, encouraged by a few cheers and catcalls, gave Marty a suggestive pouty smile, blowing him a savoury kiss as she returned to the bar. He looked as if he wanted the ground to swallow him up. "I sink she licks you." Suggested Giselle and immediately pushed back her chair and went up to the bar and immediately engaged in a hushed conversation with Madelaine. There was much smiling and furtive looks over to where the rest of us were sitting and, after a couple of minutes Giselle returned to our table. "Madelaine finis werking in serty minoots and I av ask er to join uz. I ope you don mine Danny. She say she sinks ur sweet." "Don't seem to have much choice." Mumbled Danny, under his breath. But I could tell he was feeling chuffed, after all she was quite a stunner.

The evening continued well and more beers were ordered. I was taking care not to have too much after my experience with the vino and soon started to feel a bit out of what was going on around me. True to her word Madelaine had joined us and, much to Danny's surprise and undisguised joy, sat close to him for the whole time we were there. But it was soon time for the bar to close and for us to head back. We were the last to leave and I made the effort to go outside first – I felt like a spare prick at a wedding. As I stood there waiting for the others, I couldn't help but notice Madelaine and Danny through the window – she looked like she was trying to eat his tonsils.

Eventually he managed to untangle himself from her vice-like embrace and stumbled out of the bar with the others. "Bloody hell," he spluttered, "that was some evening, what a woman!" His face was covered in lipstick and what looked like 'French mademoiselle's slobber'. "She wants to see me again tomorrow. I think I'm in love."

"Go for it Danny boy." Chorused Pete and Andy together. I didn't say a word, I was beginning to feel more out of it with every second that went by

****

We had been working on the grape farm – well what else should I call it – for around two weeks. The weather had been really hot and sunny and I had managed to get quite a tan, I was starting to look like a native! But it had its' downside because it was back breaking work and, although Jean-Claude had been good to his word and paid us a reasonable wage I was beginning to get itchy feet.

Over the past week we had worked from dawn to mid-afternoon, had a lie down before dinner and then headed to the village bar. And I suppose that was the real problem, I was the odd one out!! Pete and Andy were tied up with Jean-Claude's sisters, while Danny was falling in love with Madelaine. Of course, everyone recognised my lonely situation and Madelaine, sweet girl, had attempted to team me up with one of her friends. That was ok but I wasn't really interested, Lucille was great company, but I couldn't get over her buck teeth and lazy right eye! The problem came when she stared at me, her eye would slowly drift out and I found myself following it to see what she had found so interesting to look at. After the second evening she had taken Madelaine to one side complaining that she thought I was bored. I tried to reassure them both that it wasn't the case, but I didn't have the courage to tell them the truth.

After that the others left me to my own devices and, while I didn't want to upset Dan, I knew that it was time, for me at least, to move on. The opportunity came a few days later. A further six students had arrived later that day and I volunteered to help them settle in while Dan and the others headed into Vaux for the evening. When all was quiet, I returned to my bed and settled down to sort out my finances which, while they had received a boost from the grape picking, still continued to dwindle down slowly. It was around eleven by the time Danny wandered into the bunkhouse, I was still awake. "Have a good night mate?" I mumbled none too enthusiastically. "Yeah, it was great," came the response, "I left early cos her dad wants her to go with him tomorrow to get some stuff for the bar, so she wanted an early night. I left Pete'n Andy with the girls, didn't want to play gooseberry."

"Don't think I don't know how you feel," I couldn't help feeling spiteful, "anyhow, I've been thinking, we've been here for a while and this can't last forever. I reckon it's time for us, or me at least, to think about heading back. What d'you reckon?"

His response when it came was a bit of a surprise, "Yeah I know, I've bin thinkin' the same. I promised mum and dad we'd only be away for about a month and it's nearly that now. Don't wanna go back, it's good here, but all good things come to an end. Let's just have a few more days, ok?"

"Ok, well what say we speak to Jean-Claude in the morning and head off in a couple of days. He knew we were only going to be her for a couple of weeks anyway so it won't come as any surprise. I also reckon that Pete and Andy are going to be here for a while, certainly all the time the girls are around." So that was settled.

The following morning as I reached for a second croissant from the large bowl set in the middle of the table, Jean-Claude came in to join the throng of new students filling the kitchen. He was in his element as the vast majority of the newcomers were French.

"Bonjour mes amis, ca vas? Eh bien aujourd'hui nous allons dans les vignes et je vais te montrer ce que tu dois faire'

"I had to stop him before he got carried away "Pardon Jean-Claude," I had to raise my voice to be heard above the enthusiastic chatter around me, "Excuse me please!" I shouted, the room went quiet. "Jean-Claude, I have to tell you that Danny and I will be leaving in a couple of days. We need to return to England, we need to get ready to go back to school."

'Bugger', I thought as soon as I said it, it made me feel like we were a couple of little kids in front of all these grown-ups, but nobody seemed to notice so I breathed an inward sigh of relief.

"Oh merde!!" exclaimed Jean-Claude, forgetting himself in front of the others, particularly his mum who shot him a stony look, "I wus opping ewe wud be ear to elp uz shew zee newuns ow tu werk zee raisins."

"We'll be here for a couple of days," I quickly retorted, "so we'll do as much as we can to help."

"Ok, je comprends," came the reply. The hang-dog expression told me a different story I think he was really going to miss us.

"We're not going," chipped in Pete, "we're happy to stay around for a couple more weeks, we're enjoying it."

'Yeah right', I thought to myself, 'and we know what bits you're enjoying most'. I caught his sly wink at Andy. Jean-Claude's smiled returned immediately, Pete's offer had done the trick! "I sank ewe fer ur elp, Martee et Dannee, I ope ewe ave ad un god tim wizz uz. Mebee I av tu go tu Lyons Samedi. I ken tak ewe tu moterwhey if ewe wont?"

"That would be great," said Danny, "that gives us four more days here and save us worrying about lifts." He stared at me pleadingly, knowing I wanted to go as soon as we could.

"Yeah ok," I relented, "four more days and then we definitely leave."

The following day saw us working alongside the newcomers. They were a mixture, most coming from one university or another from various places around France. I guessed that this was a regular way of earning extra money during their summer break as they didn't need anywhere near as much help finding their way around the vines as me and Danny needed when we started.

I found myself working alongside Hanne, she had sidled across to where I was waiting to head off into the fields. I found out that she was only part-French and had been born in Sweden where she had lived until her mum and dad had split up and her mum had returned to France. We spent the morning together working the vines, she was one of the only ones not having worked on the vineyards before, so I felt quite good about showing her the ropes.

Danny didn't seem too bothered that I wasn't working with him, in fact I had noticed that he seemed to avoid me, if he could, almost like he was better than me, more grown up. It was beginning to make me feel like we were drifting apart since he had found Madelaine and I had started wondering whether I had made the right decision about suggesting we come to France. Was it that or was I just jealous?

After dinner, that evening, the whole group of us headed into Vaux and packed out the bar. I had a great time and felt happier to be with Hanne and the others, rather sitting on my own watching Danny's teeth being cleaned by Madelaine's tongue!!

Just before eleven Madelaine's dad came over and switched off the juke box which had been playing continuously for the whole evening. We needed no further reminder that he wanted to close up and, along with the others, I made ready to leave. I looked around for Danny but couldn't see any sign of him so headed off with the rest.

Hanne held onto my hand on the walk back saying that it was too dark and she wanted to make sure she didn't lose her way. We had both drunk a little too much and when we arrived back she gave me a warm kiss goodnight, promising to see me in the morning before we both headed off to our beds.

****

I felt myself being roughly prodded in the arm. "Marty wake up, come on wake up!" I struggled to open my eyes as I heard Danny's voice hissing close to my ear, "Wake up, I've got something to tell you."

"Can't it wait?" I mumbled, "what's the bloody time?"

"Don't worry about the time mate," came the response, "this can't wait till the morning. I've done it!"

"Wha'," I tried to get my brain into gear, it was proving to be a bit of an uphill struggle, "what're you on about, done what?"

"*It*!! I've done it with Madelaine," there was an unmistakable sound of triumph in his voice, "up in her room. We nipped up while her mum was in the kitchen and her dad was busy looking after you lot in the bar.

She got me in there and, before I knew it, she had me on the bed and was ripping into my jeans."

I was now fully awake, "yeah right," I mumbled, "so you lost your cherry, fat chance, pull the other one."

"No really, I'm not kidding you. We really did it, I'm not lying Marty, honestly. She got me on the bed, stripped me off and then herself. It was amazing mate, honestly no kidding!"

"So, what about a durex then?" I was reminded of what happened with me and Marie-France on the beach in Fouras, "you didn't have any, so what did you do about that?" I figured I had him there.

"She had some," he replied, "Look here's the empty packet, I'm keeping this as souvenir! It was bloody amazing mate, absolutely bloody amazing! Better'n havin' a wank any day." He pulled the torn packet out of his pocket and wave it triumphally under my nose. "Need any more proof Marty? I've cracked it. It was bloody amazing!" He stood up and sidled over to his own bed, "time for bed, Oh! I've already been to bed once already this evening."

I suddenly realised that my right hand had been cupped around my goolies and, quietly as I could, moved it away. There was no way I wanted him to think that I may have been up to something. I could hear the smirk in his voice, even though I couldn't see his face clearly. He was going to play this for all he was worth. I could see that the next few days were going to be pretty unbearable. "Go to sleep Danny," I hissed.

The following morning, I woke and got up as quickly and quietly as I could. Danny was the last person I wanted to see or talk to. He was still fast asleep and looked

like he was reliving the last evenings' events in his sleep if the smug look on his face was anything to go by. I dressed quickly and headed across to the house where some of the others had already congregated waiting patiently for coffee and croissants.

Hanne was sitting chatting to one of the other girls, but when she saw me come into the kitchen, made her excuses and came over to me. "Bonjour Martee, ow are you? Did you sleep well? We ad good time at the bar, yes?"

"Yes thanks," I replied, "it was good fun yesterday evening, would you like to go into the village again this evening?"

"Oh yeah, that would be great!" she replied, "let's make planz for zis evning when we are in ze vines," she smiled shyly, "ahh I sink le petit dejeuner is ready, let's eat."

We scrambled to the chairs, vying for the seats nearest to the huge baskets of bread and croissants. I looked up just in time to see Danny at the door, he looked around, spotted me sitting next to Hanne and strolled across. "Couldn't you wake me, idiot!!" it was a sort of superior sneer.

"Nah I figured you may need the extra rest after your supposed evening of passion,"

"Haa! That's it, you're jealous. Never mind you'll lose your cherry one day." He whispered in my ear while looking around the table to see who was watching. He was disappointed as everyone was busy feeding their bellies ready for the busy day ahead.

With breakfast over we all gathered outside ready to head off to the vines. I took the opportunity to sidle over the Dan. "Look mate we've got two days left here and then we're on our way, or at least I am. I'm going to leave it up to you whether you come with me or not."

"Yeah ok, I know I'll be coming," came the reply, "I'm sorry I didn't mean to piss you off. Let's have a couple more days and then go, ok?"

Dan and I put our differences behind us and agreed that we wouldn't interfere in what either of us got up to while we remained on the farm.

The last couple of evenings were the best of the time we had spent in Vaux. Dan spent his with Madelaine and Hanne and I were getting on well, although apart from holding hands and a couple of secretive kissing sessions, we kept our supposed relationship very much on the innocent level.

On our day of departure, we were all gathered around the kitchen table when Jean-Claude came bustling in. "Bonjour mes amis", he sounded very jolly, was he pleased to be getting rid of us, had we done something to piss him off? I quickly dismissed that thought from my mind. "Aujourd hui oi 'ave tugo antu Lyons end oivil be tak'n Merty end Daanneee wivme. Zey vilbee reeetournin 'om tuconteeinu wizerr stoodeees. Oi 'ope ewe 'ave eeenjoy zeetam ewe 'ave zpen ere wizzuz und oi ope ewe ave un zaaef journeee bakome." Jean-Claude stood looking at Dan and me, I figured he was half-expecting some sort of response.

I stood up, pushing away the bowl of coffee into which I had just been about to dunk in my second croissant, "Yeah it's been really great here and getting to know you all over the past coupla weeks. But time we were heading back home so thanks and maybe we'll see some of you again." I sat myself down quickly, feeling my face redden, and dug my croissant into the bowl.

There was a muted clapping of a couple of hands and some table banging before everyone's attention was drawn back to the important matter of filling their bellies before a hard morning in the vine fields.

We had more or less packed our rucksacks the previous evening so, after breakfast, went back to the bunkhouse to quickly finish up and get ready for the road ahead and uncertain lifts back to Cherbourg, or whatever port we decided to head for.

****

"Ferwell mi friens eatas been un grat toim veavad geteng tuno ewe. Oiop ewe av un saf journeee bak tuur oe. Maibeee vevil meat ewe igan wenewe ave feenisd ur stuudeees."

Jean-Claude jumped back into his car, having shaken our hands furiously, and disappeared in a cloud of dust as he headed off on to the motorway, heading south to Lyon. He had dropped us at the start of a slip road which led onto the motorway heading north, a long journey lay ahead of us, how much time it would take was anyone's guess.

****

The ferry butted its' way through the harbour mouth into an uncertain few hours of, what looked to be, a pretty rough sea waiting to swallow us into its' watery arms. I stared fearfully at what awaited us beyond the harbour wall. I felt my belly wrench as the front of the ferry heaved up as the first wave hit. Down we went and then back up even before I had a chance to catch my breath. Then it happened, a sudden wave of dizziness and the burning feeling in my throat. Another sweeping rise of the boat before dropping down again and this time my brow was sweating or was it the cold salt spray cutting into my face. My guts turned over and I said goodbye by to my baguette and cheese that I had enjoyed a couple of hours earlier!

I wasn't alone, already there were several others praying for calmer waters along the ferry's rail. Danny on the other hand was leaning back in the lee of the wind and spray enjoying a cigarette and a bag of crisps. He held out the packet in a sadistic gesture of offering me a crisp, I responded with the flick of a V-sign before leaning back over and discharging another jet of vomit.

I tried to think back over the last few days, trying to take my mind of what was happening. We had been quite lucky. After we had said our goodbyes to Jean-Claude at the motorway we had to wait for just a few minutes before managing to thumb down our first car for the return journey. A salesman travelling back north to Dijon broke the back of the journey back to the coast and set us down on the road to Paris. After that a few more shorter lifts and we ended up back at Le Havre where I knew we would be able to get a ferry back to Southampton and eventually home!

What a relief as the ferry rounded the Isle of Wight and entered the relative calm of the Solent. I began to feel better almost immediately and determined to leave the boat as a seasoned sea traveller and not a weakling landlubber which I knew I really was.

"Fancy a quick bite down in the café?" I ventured to Dan. I knew he was always up for anything to eat and I was starving.

"Yeah sure suits me, though I dunno whether there'll be much left at this time."

How wrong he was, the journey had obviously put a lot of people off eating and we both enjoyed a round of cheese and onion sandwiches, washed down by a couple of cokes. Just what we needed for the last leg of our journey home.

****

"Mornin' gents, so what 'ave yew got to declare, hmm?" The officious looking grot stared down at us from underneath the peak of his cap – it made me wonder if the top of his head was flat as the peak almost hid his eyes. "Any contraband stashed away in the bags of yors, any fags any whiskey?" he smirked.

I kicked Dan, warning him to keep his sarcastic comments to himself before answering on behalf of us both. "Err hello officer no we've just been on holiday for a couple of weeks to help us learn a little more of the French language you see we are both hoping to study French at A-Level we want to be able to speak the language really well because we both want to work for the Civil Service like you so we can meet lots of interesting people like you do." I paused for breath I felt if I tried to utter another word I would have passed out.

"OK smart arse, go on oppit!"

We needed no second bidding and scuttled out of the customs house into the fresh air of a Southampton afternoon.

We had made our way of the city, bent theatrically under the weight of the rucksacks, hoping that a good Samaritan would spot us and take pity on our plight.

We didn't have long to wait and when it happened, it took us both by surprise.

"Good afternoon gentlemen where are you off to?"

My mouth gaped open in astonishment, there they were the old vicar and Edith his elderly wife!! "Err we're heading for Midhampton, we've just got off the ferry from France. I don't think he remembered us.

"France eh," came the reply, "well, yes, I think we can help you young chaps out, we're heading that way too. Come on Edith, jump out," he said to his elderly and somewhat large spouse, "let the boys get into the back."

Edith opened the door and smiled up at me, "you'll have to give me a bit of help please dear." She extracted her rather large, cumbersome, legs from the foot-well and reached out her hand for me to grab hold of. I gingerly pulled her up but, with combined sweaty palms, our hands parted company just as she almost reached the full vertical position and she fell back into her seat with an oomph and a cackle of laughter from her husband still sitting inside the car. At the same time, I was greeted with an eye-full of brown stocking tops, kept in place by wide elastic suspenders cutting into ample white thighs!

Was this déjà vu? – no, in fact the very same thing happened earlier in this book!!

"So, where have you boys been to in France and what did you get up to?" asked the reverend, after we had managed to squeeze ourselves into the back of the old Anglia, "Did you managed to score with any of those lovely French fillies? I remember the days just after D-Day when I was a young army chaplain, ministering unto the boys in our unit, they told me some stories I can tell you! In fact, I ministered, not only to their emotional needs but also their physical ones – being the main source for the distribution of protectives." He looked into his rear-view mirror and gave a knowing wink.

"Now then Henry, don't you go corrupting those young men with your wartime stories," admonished his wife with a cheery smile, "they will have plenty of time in the future to get to know some nice English gals without having to cross the Channel to France." She gently massaged his neck and shoulders.

Danny nudged me sharply in the ribs "wotsy onabout protectives?" he mouthed.

"Durex!!" I mouthed back, doubt beginning to course through my mind as to whether he had actually lost his virginity to Madelaine.

Thirty minutes later we waved goodbye to the oldies after once again having to struggle out of the little car together with our, by now, rather tatty looking rucksacks.

"Well, looks like that's it for this year," murmured Danny, "back to the old routine of school, exams and all that crap."

"Yeah, it's been quite an adventure," I replied, "but I'm glad we did it, certainly got a few things to brag about when we see the others, that's a fact. You glad we did it?"

"You bet I am. Certainly got a bug for the hitching that's for sure. We'll have to think about where to go next year," said Dan, "can't just leave it as only one trip away, we need to see the world." He waved his arm around expansively, "there's a whole lotta places we need to see and things to do. I've got the bug for travel and women." He gave me a knowing wink and I tried to dismiss the memory of his bragging back at the vineyard – would he ever let me forget about the night he lost his cherry?

We wandered into the centre of town hoping that we may meet up with a few mates, but it was after closing time and the place was empty, so we said a hasty goodbye and set off in the direction of our respective homes.

I cautiously opened the back door and crept into the kitchen, the aroma of a tasty dinner, freshly prepared, filled my nostrils and I knew straight away that I was glad to be back home. "Hi it's me," I called out as I went into the hall.

"In here," I heard mum call back, "we're in the dining room."

Before I could answer, the dining room door flew open and mum rushed through throwing her arms around me "Oh Martin, it's so good to see you. Arrgghhh! You need a good wash. You're not sitting down here smelling like that, get up those stairs and run yourself a bath."

I was home!

"Give the boy a chance luv," said dad as, he too, came to the door, "the wanderer returns, how are you boy, have a good time?

"Brilliant," I replied, "definitely going to do it again next year, may even go for a bit longer."

"Well, you've been away a few weeks this time," reminded mum, "so let's just wait and see what next year brings. Don't forget that you get your O-level results in a few days and if you've not got your grades to do your A-levels then you'll be looking for a job."

"OK," I grumbled, "I'll go a run a bath."

"Well don't be too long Martin," mum called after me as I headed for the stairs, "I'll have your dinner ready, and I've got some news for you too."

My heart skipped a beat, what sort of news? What have I done? I've only been home five minutes. I sought the sanctity of my bedroom, somewhere where I could gather my thoughts about what I was soon to be told. Questions flurried through my mind, anything that I may or may not be guilty of must have happened weeks before. Despite racking my brains, I could think of nothing. Then I remembered why I had been sent upstairs and ran myself a bath.

Fifteen minutes later, having cleaned up the brown tidemark of scum from around the bath I went downstairs to learn my fate. Both mum and dad were in the kitchen, mum washing up the dinner things while dad was drying. Mum turned round and admiring my tidier appearance said, "I've left your dinner in the oven, have it now before it dries out too much. I expect you're looking forward to a square meal, can't imagine you boys ate too much wholesome food while you were away, eh?"

"You're right there, mum," I replied and headed straight to where my much needed dinner was waiting.

I took my plate of steaming food, roast beef, cabbage, spuds and carrots, into the dining room where little brother was still sitting at the table indulging in his favourite pastime – picking his nose. "Still hungry Brian?" I enquired.

"Nice to see you too," came the less than welcoming response as he slid off his chair and stomped out of the room with not so much as a backward glance. Eleven-year-olds can be such a pain in the arse I thought.

"Are you enjoying that love?" asked mum, wiping her hands on a tea towel as she came in from the kitchen.

"You bet," I replied before stuffing another roastie into my mouth, "didn't realise I was so hungry."

"Well, you can't beat a good old roast dinner," she replied, "they don't do meals like that over in France do they."

I nodded my reply as my mouth was stuffed full. I took a quick swallow, "Errrr, so what have you got to tell me, what have I done." I couldn't disguise the belligerent fear in my voice.

"Ah yes, well, I met Bert Matthews a few days ago and mentioned that we were expecting you back in a couple of weeks. He was saying that they were a bit short of workers at the moment and, if you like, he could give you a job up to the end of the school holidays."

I sat there staring at her, I didn't know what to say until I blurted out, "What that bloke who works down Budd's Farm?"

"Well, actually, he's the manager down there and is employing students over the holidays. As he said to me it gives them a bit of pocket money and also keeps them out of trouble." She eye'd me accusingly.

"But I haven't done anything wrong mum, have I? And Budd's Farm!! The bloody sewage works!! Who would want to work there?"

"Now then young man! Don't let me hear you speaking to your mother like that again. You're not too old to go over my knee you know. We've talked about you working there and, I agree with your mum, a spell working down there for just a few weeks until you go back to school would do you the world of good. And another thing, we raised no objection about you going off to France for a few weeks. We could have but our foot down and said no to that, but we didn't so now I think it's time you did something to earn a few bob."

So that was how I went from working in the vine fields of central France, picking grapes which went into the making of the classic Beaujolais wine to shovelling shit in a sewage works just outside of Portsmouth! My days, through to the end of my school holidays, started at 7:30 with a half hour for lunch. Every morning mum sent me off with a peck on the cheek, a round of cheese and pickle sandwiches, an apple and a bag of crisps together, of course, with a cheery wave goodbye and a "have a lovely day darling."

The work wasn't too bad and together with the other students, there were 6 of us, we managed to alleviate the boredom by the occasional sludge fight while we waited for the trailer to be drawn up next to the bay. We then had to shovel out the sludge for it to be taken for processing into fertiliser. Of course, the best day of the week was Friday when we queued up outside the pay office to collect our weeks wages – six pounds seven and six.

Exam results day came round quickly and I asked mum if she wouldn't mind calling Bert Matthews to tell him that I wouldn't be able to get into work at the usual time. "Of course, love, in fact I'll ask him if you can take the day off to be able to celebrate your results." Mum was the eternal optimist!

I headed off to school joining up with Danny and the others as we pushed our way into the school hall where a some of the teachers were sitting around behind a few tables assembled in a semi-circle around the edge of the hall, leaving us hanging round wondering what was going to happen next. Finally Tubby Jackson, the deputy head slapped a heavy hand on one of the tables to bring the room to order. "Good morning everyone and welcome to results day. I hope you have had a wonderful, few weeks break and, I'm sure, you're looking forward to finding out how you have done in your exams. We've arranged the results envelopes on these tables in alphabetical order," he waved his arm dramatically around the room, "so if I could ask you to form an orderly queue at your respective tables, the first one will be A to E and so on, a member of staff will hand you your results envelope."

I shuffled forward and before I knew what was happening a buff envelope was shoved in my hand by Miss Thompson with a murmured "Well done Danny, I hope you had a lovely time on your travels through France." She had remembered and I'd forgotten to send her a card!

"Thanks Miss," I retorted and slunk away to find a quiet corner. My hands were shaking as I tore out the envelope and pulled out the flimsy sheet of paper inside. I quickly scanned through the results, not really able to take it all in. I couldn't believe my luck, with the exception of English Lit I had got all the grades I needed to carry on in the sixth form – another two years at school!!

I searched out the others and we all did a quick comparison. Danny and I would be staying on, only Frank Dedman would be leaving to do an apprenticeship, but that was what he wanted in any case. Having agreed to meet up later in the middle of town we made our separate ways home.

As I turned down onto our front path I saw the curtains in the lounge twitch and, before I reached the house mum had opened the door with a wide smile across her face.

"Well?" she smiled, "how did you get on love?"

"Really well mum," I replied, "I got all the grades I need so will be staying on to do my A's."

"That's wonderful news love, and I have some news for you too." I looked at her quizzically. "You have a visitor waiting in the lounge, a young lady, she says her name is Marie-France!" She smiled.

The End

Printed in Great Britain
by Amazon